The Body Where I Was Born

The Body Where I Was Born

a novel

GUADALUPE NETTEL

translated from the Spanish by
J. T. Lichtenstein

Seven Stories Press
NEW YORK • OAKLAND

Seven Stories Press
140 Watts Street
New York, NY 10013
www.sevenstories.com

College professors may order examination copies of Seven Stories Press titles for free. To order, visit http://www.sevenstories.com/textbook or send a fax on school letterhead to (212) 226-1411.

Book design by Elizabeth DeLong

Library of Congress Cataloging-in-Publication Data
Nettel, Guadalupe, 1973-
    [Cuerpo en que nací. English]
    The body where I was born / Guadalupe Nettel ; translated by J.T. Lichtenstein. -- A Seven Stories Press first edition.
        pages cm
    "First English-language edition" -- Verso title page.
    Originally published as El cuerpo en que nací. Barcelona : Editorial Anagrama, 2011.
    ISBN 978-1-60980-526-5 (hardback)
    1. Domestic fiction. 2. Psychological fiction. I. Lichtenstein, J. T., 1986- translator. II. Title.
    PQ7298.424.E76C8415 2015
    863'.7--dc23
                                        2015006198

Printed in the United States

9 8 7 6 5 4 3 2 1

For Lorenzo and Mateo

yes, yes,
        that's what
I wanted,
        I always wanted,
I always wanted,
        to return
to the body
        where I was born.

ALLEN GINSBERG, "Song"

I.

I was born with a white beauty mark, or what others call a birthmark, covering the cornea of my right eye. That spot would have been nothing had it not stretched across my iris and over the pupil through which light must pass to reach the back of the brain. They didn't perform cornea transplants on newborns in those days; the spot was doomed to remain for several years. And in the same way an unventilated tunnel slowly fills with mold, the pupillary blockage led to the growth of a cataract. The only advice the doctors could give my parents was to wait: by the time their daughter finished growing, medicine would surely have advanced enough to offer the solution they now lacked. In the meantime, they advised subjecting me to a series of annoying exercises to develop, as much as possible, the defective eye. This was done with ocular movements similar to those Aldous Huxley suggests in *The Art of Seeing*, but also—and this I remember most—with a patch that covered my left eye for half the day. It was a piece of flesh-colored cloth with sticky, adhesive edges, covering my upper eyelid down to the top of my cheekbone. At first glance, it looked like I had no eye, only a smooth surface there. Wearing the patch felt unfair and oppressive. It was hard to let them put it on me every morning and to accept that no hiding place and no amount of crying could save me from that torture. I don't think there was a single day I didn't resist. It would have been so easy to wait until they left me at the school entrance to yank the patch off with the same careless gesture I used to tear scabs off my knee. But for some reason I still can't understand, I never tried to remove it.

With the patch, I had to go to school, identify my teacher and the shapes of my school supplies, come home, eat, and play for part of the afternoon. At around five o'clock, someone would come to say it was time to take it off, and with these words I would return to the world of clarity and precise shapes. The people and things around me suddenly changed. I could see far into the distance and would become mesmerized by the treetops and infinite leaves that composed them, the contours of the clouds in the sky, the tint of the flowers, the intricate pattern of my fingertips. My life was divided between two worlds: that of morning, built mostly out of sounds and smells, but also of hazy colors; and that of evening, always freeing, yet at the same time, overwhelmingly precise.

Given the circumstances, school was a place even more inhospitable than those institutions often are. I couldn't see much, but it was enough to know how to get around within the labyrinth of hallways, fences, gardens. I liked climbing the trees. My hyperdeveloped tactile sense allowed me to easily distinguish the firm branches from the frail, and to know which cracks in the trunk made the best footholds. The real problem wasn't so much the place as it was the other children. We knew there were many differences between us; they stayed away from me, and I from them. My classmates would ask, suspiciously, what the patch was hiding—it had to be something terrifying if it needed to be covered—and when I wasn't paying attention, they would reach with their grubby little hands, trying to touch it. Alone, my right eye made them curious and uncomfortable. Sometimes now, at the ophthalmologist's office or at a bench in the park, I cross paths with a patched child and recognize in them the anxiety so characteristic of my childhood. It keeps them from being still. I know it's how they face danger—it's evidence of good survival instincts. They're on edge because they can't stand the idea that a cloudy world should slip through their fingers. They have to explore, find a way to own it. There were no other children at my school like me, but I did have classmates with other kinds of abnormalities. I remember a dwarf, a redheaded girl with a cleft lip, a boy with leukemia who left us before elementary school was over, and a very sweet girl who was a paralytic. Together we shared the certainty that we were not the same as the others and that we knew this life better than the horde of innocents who in their brief existence had yet to face any kind of misfortune.

My parents and I visited ophthalmologists in New York, Los Angeles, and Boston, and also in Barcelona and Bogota, where the famous Barraquer brothers worked. In each of these places, the same diagnosis resounded like a macabre echo repeating itself, postponing the solution until a hypothetical future. The doctor we most often visited worked at the ophthalmology hospital in San Diego, just across the border where my father's sister also lived. His name was John Pentley and he was a good-natured little old man who zealously prepared potions and prescribed eye drops. He gave my parents a greasy ointment to smear into my eye every morning. He also prescribed atropine drops, a substance that dilates the pupil to its maximum size and that made my world dazzle, turning reality into a cosmic interrogation room. The same doctor advised exposing my eyes to black light. For this, my parents built a wooden box that my small head fit into perfectly, then they lit it up. In the background, like a primitive cinemascope, drawings of animals went around and around: a deer, a turtle, a bird, a peacock. This routine would take place in the afternoon. Immediately after that, they would remove the patch. Recounted in this way, it might all sound amusing, but living through it was agonizing. There are people who are forced to study a musical instrument during their childhood, or to train for gymnastic competitions; me, I trained to see with the same discipline others use to prepare for futures as professional athletes.

But sight was not my family's only obsession. My parents seemed to think of childhood as the preparatory phase in which they had to correct all the manufacturing defects one enters the world with, and they took this job very seriously. I remember the afternoon when, during a consultation with an orthopedist—clearly lacking any knowledge of child psychology—it occurred to him to declare that my hamstrings were too short, and that this explained my tendency to curve my spine as if trying to protect myself. When I look at photos from those days, it seems to me the curvature in question was barely perceptible in profile. Much more noticeable is my expression: a tense smile, much like the smile that can be detected in some of the photographs Diane Arbus took of children in the suburbs of New York. Nevertheless, my mother took it on as a personal challenge to correct my posture, which she often referred to using animal metaphors. And so, from then on, in addition to the exercises to strengthen my right eye, a series of leg stretches was incorporated into my daily routine. My habit looked so much to her like curling into a shell that she came up with a nickname, a term of endearment, which she claimed perfectly matched my way of walking.

"Cucaracha!" she yelled every two to three hours. "Stand up straight!" Or, "Cucaracha, it's time for your atropine drops!"

I want you to tell me plain and simple, Dr. Sazlavski, if a human being can make it out of such a regimen unharmed? And if so, why didn't I? If we really look at it, it's not so strange. Many people during their childhoods suffer corrective treatment in response to nothing more than their parents' more or less arbitrary obsessions. "Don't speak like that, speak like this." "Don't eat like that, eat like this." "Don't do such things, do other such things." "Don't think that, think this." Perhaps therein lies the true rule of the conservation of our species. We perpetuate unto the newest generation the neuroses of our forbearers, wounds we keep inflicting on ourselves like a second layer of genetic inscription.

At about halfway through all this training, an important event took place in our structured family life: one afternoon, not long before summer vacation, my mother brought Lucas into the world, a blond and chubby boy, who took up most of her attention and who was able to distract her from her corrective agenda, for a few months at least. I will not talk too much about my brother. It is not my intention to tell or interpret his story, just as it does not interest me to tell or interpret anyone's story but my own. Still, unfortunately for him and for my parents, a good part of his life intertwines with mine. Even so, I want to be clear that the origin of this tale lies in the need to understand certain events and certain dynamics that formed this complex amalgam—this mosaic of images, memories, and emotions—that breathes within me, remembers with me, entwines others, and takes refuge in a pencil the way others take refuge in drinking or gambling.

One summer, Dr. Pentley finally announced that we could stop the daily use of the patch. According to him, my optic nerve had developed to its maximum potential. All that was left was to wait until I had finished growing and they would be able to operate on me. Even though nearly thirty years have passed since then, I haven't forgotten that moment. It was a fresh morning full of sun. My parents, brother, and I walked out of the clinic hand-in-hand. There was a park nearby where we went in search of ice cream, like the normal family we would be—at least we dreamed we would be—from that point on. We could congratulate ourselves; our resistance had won us the battle.

Of the good times I had with my family, I remember in

particular the weekends we spent together at our country house in the state of Morelos, one hour outside Mexico City. My father had bought the land just after my brother was born and built the house my mother designed with the help of a prestigious architect. Carried away by who knows what romantic fantasies, they also built a barn and horse stable. But the only animals we ended up having were a German Shepherd and a good number of hens that kept themselves busy laying eggs. As much as I pleaded, I never convinced my parents to buy lambs or ponies. Our relationship with Betty, our weekend dog, was as loving as it was distant. We never felt the responsibility to train her, to take her out for walks, or to feed her, so even though she was affectionate with us, her canine loyalty belonged to the gardener. Behind the farmhouse ran a clear stream where we'd swim and use plastic bags to catch tadpoles and axolotls, those mysterious animals Cortázar might have mythologized in a short story. My brother and I would spend more than five hours a day in the water, wearing rubber boots and bathing suits. Now, thirty years later, it is impossible to swim in that stream; it's filled with excrement and toxic residue. One of the wonderful things about that house was the abundance of fruit trees, especially mango trees, lemon trees, and avocado trees. When we'd return to the city, we often brought boxes of avocados in the car to sell to our neighbors. My brother and I were in charge of this job, and it was how we scraped together a decent savings to be squandered over the holidays.

Around that time—I must have been starting third grade—I started to develop a reading habit. I began reading a few years before, but now that I had unlimited access to the clear universe—to which belonged the words and pictures of children's books—I decided to take advantage of it. I mostly read short stories, but also a few longer books by the likes of Wilde and Stevenson. I preferred suspense or scary stories, *The Picture of Dorian Gray* or *The Bottle Imp*. I often read the equally or even more terrifying stories in my father's book of Bible legends. There was Princess Salome who beheaded the man she so desired, there was Daniel thrown into the lion's den. Writing was the natural next step. In my lined notebooks, the French kind, I wrote down tales in which my classmates were protagonists who went to faraway lands where every kind of calamity befell them. Those stories were my opportunity for revenge, and I was not going to waste it. It wasn't long before the teacher caught on and, moved by some strange solidarity, decided to organize a literary assembly where I could express myself. I refused to read unless I knew beforehand that an adult would stay by my side until my parents came to pick me up that afternoon, since it was very possible that more than one of my classmates would be looking to settle a score after class. As it happened, things turned out differently than I expected. After reading a story in which six of my classmates tragically died trying to escape from an Egyptian pyramid, there was enthusiastic applause. Those who had been featured in the story smugly came up to congratulate me, and those who had not been featured begged me to make them characters in my next tale. That was how, little by little, I earned my particular place at school. I had not stopped being marginalized, but it wasn't oppressive anymore.

It was the seventies, and my family had embraced some of the prevailing progressive ideas of the time. I went to one of the few Montessori schools in Mexico City (today there's one on every corner). I know that in those days there were institutions where kids could literally do whatever they felt like. They could set their classrooms on fire and not go to jail or suffer any severe punishment. In my school, we had neither absolute freedom nor stifling discipline. There were no blackboards, no desk chairs set up to face the teacher who, naturally, did not answer to that name, but to "guide." Each kid worked at a real table—a desk that was all ours, at least for a year—on which we were allowed to leave distinctive marks, drawings and stickers, so long as we didn't damage the desks beyond repair. Against the walls were bookcases and shelves where we kept our work supplies: wooden jigsaw puzzles of maps with all the world's countries and flags; multiplication tables that looked like Scrabble boards; textured letters; bells of various sizes; geometric shapes made out of metal; laminated papers with different parts of the human anatomy and their names, to mention a few. Before we could use anything, we had to ask our guide for instructions. It didn't really matter what we did during the morning, we just had to work on something, or at least pretend to work. A few times a year there were parties for all the families, and then you could really measure the havoc the seventies had wreaked. Guests at these parties included kids whose parents lived in three-way partnerships or other polygamous situations, and instead of feeling ashamed, they flaunted it. The names of some of my classmates give another eloquent vestige of those years. Some of them reflected ideological leanings, like "Krouchevna," "Lenin," and even "Supreme Soviet" (we nicknamed him "the Viet"). Others spoke to religious beliefs, like "Uma" or "Lini," whose full name honored India's snake of cosmic energy. Others, still, spoke to more personal devotions, like "Clitoris." That was the name of a lovely and innocent girl, the daughter of an infrarealist writer, who did not yet comprehend the wrong her parents had done her and who, to her misfortune, didn't have a nickname.

Among the strange policies my parents imposed was one about never lying to us. This was an absurd decision, from my point of view, which they were able to commit to for years, but only on a handful of not-so-essential fronts, including the way babies are made, the uselessness of religion, and Santa Clause, in whom we were never allowed to believe. Living under these conditions stuck us at the margin of our society; if at some age it's possible to enjoy the ominous season that comes around at the end of every year—carolers at the supermarket, decorated pine trees in the windows, and everything else that creates the so-called "magic of Christmas"—we were deprived of it. Every time a fat man with a fake beard and the unmistakable red suit appeared in the hallway of a mall we were visiting, my parents would kneel down so they could whisper in our ears that he was an imposter, "a man in a costume with no other way to earn a living." With these few words, wonderful Santa turned into a pitiful, if not pathetic soul. Our classmates, on the other hand, were allowed to believe in all the paraphernalia and naturally they enjoyed it. They innocently wrote their year-end letters, asking for this or that gift— sometimes extravagant requests their parents would fulfill down to the last detail. Several of these parents approached us after class and begged us not to give away their secret. My brother and I had to bite our tongues, resisting the enormous temptation to disenchant the others. I have to admit that I also felt a certain nostalgia for the illusion. Not being allowed to believe in Christmas stories seemed unfair to me. On the twenty-fifth of December, we would find beneath the tree the presents our parents had told us they'd be putting there during the night. There was, among the most memorable gifts, a red tricycle that I rode until I was five, and a pair of binoculars that inspired a life calling. Our apartment was in a building complex, and our neighbors' windows offered an almost limitless menu. The magnification of my binoculars wasn't very powerful, but it was enough to see close-up what went on in our vicinity. I don't know if it's what my parents had in mind, but for me the binoculars were a kind of compensation for all the time they had limited my sight with the patch. Thanks to this marvelous instrument, for years I was able to enter the homes of others and to observe things to which nobody else had access.

Another of my family's self-determining policies was to give us a sexual education free of taboos. This was mostly carried out through an open and occasionally excessively candid dialogue on the subject, but also through allegorical tales. On many nights, or in the middle of the afternoon, if the opportunity presented itself, my mother would tell me a story of her own extraordinary invention. She would explain (at least) that it was a fictional tale with educational purposes. Her very peculiar version of "Sleeping Beauty" went something like this:

One cold afternoon in winter, the queen summoned the royal physician in alarm because it had been more than two months since she had menstruated. The doctor, astonished at the naivety of his sovereign, said to her: "Her majesty must know by now that if a woman, noble or common, does not bleed for more than thirty days in a row, it is most likely that she is with child." That afternoon, the king and the queen announced the news to their subjects: very soon there would be an heir to the throne. And so it was, that in less than nine months, a beautiful little princess named Aurora was born.

What happened next: the poisoned spindle, the princess's slumber, but all the rest wasn't so important after a start like that. The story left some things unexplained. It wasn't long before it began to seem incomplete to me, and therefore troubling. What was a period, exactly? Why could a queen become pregnant? What did the womanly bleeding have to do with making a baby? The story didn't clear up any of that. My parents didn't want to lie to us, but fighting the tradition of mystery in which they had been educated turned out to be not so easy. To make their undertaking easier, they gave us a collection of books that explained the sexual anatomy of men and women in detail, as well as intercourse and the potential results thereof. But I didn't even have enough time to grasp the subject of reproduction before my parents hastened to explain that apart from that purpose genitals had other uses, recreational ones, like sex. Even if children were indeed products of coitus, the objective of such an encounter was not to engender new lives, at least not in most cases.

Instead of clarifying things, my parents made them increasingly confusing and distressing.

"So," I said, trying to recap on our way to school, from the backseat of the car, "why do people have sex?"

"To feel pleasure," the two adults seated in the front responded in unison. With my brother absorbed in his contemplation of the cars on the road, I attacked again, "But what does that mean?"

"Something that we like very much, like dancing or eating chocolate."

Eating chocolate! Hearing an answer like that, it's not unlikely a girl would want to lock herself that very morning in the school bathroom with the first boy she sees. Why didn't it occur to anyone to tell me, Dr. Sazlavski, that people have sex because they love each other and it's another way for them to show it? That might have been a bit more exact and less troubling, don't you think? I suppose that telling us all this made them feel more responsible and evolved than their own parents, and the satisfaction kept them from seeing the anxiety they were generating in my mind. I don't want to say they were wrong, but I feel that our "education" was premature (I was six) and a little overwhelming. On the other hand, my brother, who was maybe three years old at the time, was able to float above it all like a person who boards a boat twenty minutes before a tsunami hits and with innocent serenity lets the wave pass below him.

Unlike the secret of Christmas, which my brother and I did keep, I decided that nobody in my midst would be left uninformed about the business of reproduction. I even started a mural newspaper with a first edition dedicated solely to the subject. The editorial team was made up of three sisters, last name Rinaldi, whose parents were even more liberal than mine. The headmistress, a very friendly and rather lenient woman, let us put our mural newspaper up for several days. However, she was soon forced to shut us down due to complaints from more conservative parents who threatened to take their children out of the school. Other families came to our defense. It was the first time I heard talk about freedom of speech, a chimera as obsolete in my country as Quetzalcoatl, the feathered serpent.

The Rinaldi sisters had always been at my school, but we had never been in the same class. We became friends at one of the end-of-year gatherings that were held at a country house. Our parents felt an immediate kinship and decided to get together on weekends. We all traveled to Cuernavaca and Valle de Bravo. The Rinaldi girls were blond, freckled, and gifted with a surprising sense of humor. The oldest was Irene, who was in my grade but in a different group. She spent her recesses clandestinely, absorbed in her own games on the roof of the school, far from the hustle and bustle of the yard. Like me, she wasn't afraid of heights. We quickly became good friends. Her family lived on the side of the Ajusco hill, which in those days was considered outside the city. Still under construction, the house had an American kitchen, a sculpting studio where her mother worked, a dining room, and two huge lofts situated face-to-face, which served as bedrooms with neither curtains nor doors. If that wasn't enough, Irene's parents were in the habit of giving in to their sexual impulses right in front of their daughters, with no regard to what part of the house they were in. One time, I saw them going at it in the living room while I was supposed to be watching cartoons with the girls. The three sisters remained engrossed by the TV, acting as if nothing was going on. I, on the other hand, kept still as stone, intently watching the spectacle. It was a practical demonstration of the theory I had been hearing about for months. And yet, it was difficult to associate what I was seeing with my own eyes with the books on anatomy and reproduction. I wondered if, in this moment, Irene's parents were making a fourth sister, or if it was just a way for them to have a good time. But how could someone "have a good time" in such a strange way? Their movements looked more like hand-to-hand combat, like my brother's and mine when we fought over toys. Grunting, screaming, biting, Judo holds—how was this like eating chocolate? The scene was so violent that Max, the family's grouchy Pekingese with very sharp teeth, came over to try and stop it, pulling at the shirt of Gonzalo Rinaldi as he merrily mounted his wife from behind. Feeling the nip in his back, Irene's dad grimaced in pain and with a kick launched the animal into the air. Andrea, the middle daughter, burst out laughing and I couldn't help but do the same. Then

the other two sisters joined in the nervous laughter we
were unable to contain. Where are those girls today? Did
they honorably survive the seventies? I hope so, with all
my heart. But it wouldn't surprise me to learn that one of
them is now institutionalized, or that one had turned into a
prude. It is said that the extremely conservative turn taken
by the generation to which I belong is due largely in part to
the emergence of AIDS; I am convinced that our attitude
is very much a reaction to the highly experimental way our
parents confronted adulthood.

As I said before, my family lived in a residential complex
of almost twenty-five buildings. Despite that, it was a fun
place to grow up. Each building had a green area where the
social kids would get together in the afternoons to play,
while the antisocial ones would watch from a distance.
There was also a huge esplanade where kids could roller-
skate and ride bikes, and a place with swings and metal
climbing sets. In the days of the patch, I liked to climb
by myself up the ladder of the seven-foot slide, which I
would usually slide down. But more than once, I fell to the
ground from the ladder instead of sliding down the silver
slope. I was an intrepid little girl and the risks heightened
by my condition only made these games all the more thrilling. I still have a scar over my right temple from a see-saw
that refused to stop for me as I went by on my reckless way.
I sustained a similar injury from a swing that slammed into
my head at top speed, hitting just below my left earlobe.
Avenue Insurgentes marked the eastern edge of the

complex, and to the west was a sports club located in the same spot the 1968 Olympic Games took place years earlier. The facility included a running track and a hundred-meter pool. There was also a pyramid in the complex, a church—a synagogue would have better matched the makeup of the neighborhood—and a state supermarket of enormous dimensions for the time.

Of all the nooks and crannies, my favorite place was a tree right in front of my building, whose branches reached up to the apartment where we lived. It was a very old Peruvian pepper tree rooted in a mound of volcanic rocks. The width of its trunk and density of its leaves made it a spectacular tree. When I climbed it, I felt challenged and at the same time sheltered. I was sure that this tree would never let me fall from its branches, and so I climbed to the highest one with a calmness admirable to anyone watching from below. It was a sanctuary where I did not have to curve my spine to feel safe. At that age, I felt a constant need to defend myself from my environment. Instead of playing with the other kids in the plaza, I spent my afternoons with the drying racks up on the rooftops, where nobody ever went. I also preferred to reach our fifth-floor apartment by taking the back staircase instead of risking getting stuck in the elevator for hours with some neighbor. In that sense—much more than in any physical respect—I really did resemble the cockroaches that travel through the marginal spaces and buried pipes of buildings. It was as if, at some point, I had decided to build an alternative geography, a secret territory within the complex, through which to move about as I pleased, unseen.

One of my mother's sisters, the one who visited us more often than the others, and for whom I had always felt a special fondness—she was an exceptionally sensitive woman, a lover of the grotesque and the scatological, of Borges' poetry, Rabelais' novels and Goya's paintings—invented a tale inspired by my surreptitious behavior, which she would tell us at night after reading from the children's edition of *Gargantua y Pantagruel.* Her story described the adventures of Perla, a very pretty girl who suffered from terrible constipation. One afternoon, her parents set off to the grocery store for a few hours and Perla decided to remain on her potty until she could expel all the stool she has stored up in her body. Moved, perhaps, by the marvelous silence throughout the house, or by the relaxed and pleasant sensation of being alone, the poop began to come out, at first one piece at a time like little rabbit droppings, then like bland meatballs of considerable size until they spilled over the sides of the plastic receptacle on which Perla sat.

"Plop, plop," sounded the poop falling in the middle of the afternoon. The feces rolled into the bedrooms, invaded the apartment, and began to flow like a stream down the stairs of the building, then onto the sidewalks, into the courtyards of the housing complex—"Plop, plop!"—and soon it reached Avenue Insurgentes, only to flow inevitably across the entire city. The story of Perla can be seen as a cautionary tale, for it describes the situation that has come to characterize our beloved Mexico City, overcome today by faulty sewage lines and garbage dumps.

The staircase in my building had a hand in my education that my parents never imagined. It was a cool and isolated spot, with just enough light coming through a few glass-block windows. There, almost by chance, I made an important discovery about my body. It happened during one of those very hot vacation days. One of my favorite games was to leap up the clay steps two at a time and slide down the iron handrail. It was something I had done often, always innocuously. But that afternoon, for some reason I couldn't explain, the sensation felt surprisingly pleasurable. It was like a tickle just above my thigh that needed to be felt again and again, faster and faster. Everything was at contrast: the feeling of being hidden, shielded from eyes, and still in danger of someone finding me engaged in a game that somehow seemed wrong. The coolness of the rail and the heat of the friction sent an addictive shiver through my body. In seconds, those feelings opened up the gates to the heavenly world of masturbation. It was like reaching an alternate dimension or discovering a psychedelic substance. In that moment, my parents' long and boring lectures about the purpose of sex were the furthest thing from my mind. So much so, that one afternoon I innocently revealed to my mother why I spent so much time in the service stairwell, and to my surprise—and probably to yours too, Dr. Sazlavski—she didn't think it was a good idea for her daughter to masturbate in such an open place where no one ever went, even though I was doing it fully dressed while pretending to play a game. Her reaction was much closer to shame than celebration. As if what I was doing was something bad, she asked me to do "that" only in the bedroom, which of course I shared with my little brother. That's how, with the seventies in full swing, I joined the ancestral order of closet masturbators, that legion of children who rarely peak their heads out from under the sheets. But still, I should admit that I didn't completely obey. I returned to the stairs many more times than my mother ever imagined, being extra careful that no one caught me in my refreshing ritual. It surprises me still to remember the things that excited me in those early years. It was unpredictable things like words, intonations in a voice, or watching a public display of affection, but also certain sounds like the whistle of the man who sold sweet potatoes or of the man who sharpened knives. All these little nothings were calls that sent me running to the handrail or my bedroom. Sometimes I see puppies who when presented with any chance of friction will publically yield to their own expectant pleasure. That was me when I was seven years old, a little girl with an unbridled carnal appetite who would succumb to a kind of desire for furniture, armchairs, the edge of a table, the front rim of the sink, or the metal poles of the swing set.

Even though no one told me, it wasn't long before I understood that sex was not only something pleasurable like chocolate; it was also a means to hurt someone, deeply and determinately. It was my childhood habit of listening through closed doors that led to this discovery. One afternoon, our neighbor from the last apartment on the fourth floor came to visit. She was the mother of two girls who lived downstairs from us in a clean and very organized apartment with enormous fish tanks that I still remember.

Her daughters were beautiful Argentine girls with dark hair and intensely blue, catlike eyes. On several occasions we had crossed paths in the plaza and shared friendly but shy exchanges. It goes without saying that our building complex, with its seemingly bucolic gardens, also had a macabre and at times dangerous dimension. As I said before, our unit had housed the athletes of the '68 Olympics. That time and those games constitute, as the whole world knows, the symbol of the worst massacre committed in Mexico and the start of the wave of repression that characterized the continent through the next decade. And yet, as paradoxical as it might seem, these buildings were full of leftist South Americans who had come to Mexico to escape being assassinated in their own fascist countries, as my mother explained to us in a solemn tone. Back to our neighbor: I remember that on this occasion she looked haggard. My mother was very sweet with her, sat her down in the living room and offered her tea, then sharply told me to go to my room. Bit by bit, between sobs and from the clipped phrases I was able to pick up from the hallway, our neighbor explained how the day before, in the same garden where I often gave my dolls baths, a janitorial worker had abused her daughter Yanina in broad daylight. I didn't understand what had happened, but I knew the man had done something horrible and irrevocable to the girl. I also understood that despite all her pain the woman had come to tell my mother to be extra careful, to watch out so the same thing wouldn't happen to me. When our neighbor left, I tried to coax more information out of my mother, but she changed the subject. There was no human power that could convince her to explain what had happened to the girl from downstairs. It wasn't until nighttime, when my dad came home from the office and my parents thought my brother and I were asleep, that my mom told the story in full and I was able to pick up a few details. My dad agreed that it was best not to tell us anything, but they would accompany us to the plaza from then on. I was up all night crying and thinking about Yanina and how terrible sex could be, scared of suffering something similar. It was the first time I encountered a taboo, and I do understand why it went this way, but I would like you to tell me, Dr. Sazlavski, isn't the effect of silence much worse on children who are used to asking and knowing about everything? Wouldn't it have been better to tell us about the dangers lurking close-by? Or at least more pertinent than sowing confusion about things that have nothing to do with the day-to-day life of a seven-year-old? Yanina was never the same. Once a flirtatious and exceedingly feminine girl, she began to hide beneath baggy clothing and a scowl. A few months later, she cut her hair like a boy's and started to gain weight, as if she wanted to cover the prematurely developed shape of her body with fat. A few months after that, her family moved to a smaller, safer housing complex.

Sexual freedom ended up hurting my family when my parents adopted a practice very much in fashion in the seventies: the then-famous "open relationship." "Opening" the relationship basically meant doing away with exclusivity—a rule that seems to me fundamental to preserving a marriage. Based on a mutual agreement, of which, I stress, my brother and I were never informed, my parents had the right to go out and sleep with anyone—to ride all around town. Doctor, why didn't they tell us? Maybe they weren't totally convinced of the benefits of their new rule, or perhaps they realized they had already gone too far on the topic of sex with us. What they did do was introduce us to a wide variety of new friends who showed up at the house, said hello, and left almost as quickly as they came. In very little time—quickened by my habit of listening through walls—I learned about the new situation and, of course, immediately told my brother. They justified their decision to other grownups with the argument that private property was scandalous and, if they couldn't do away with it completely, they could at least do their part by making their bodies accessible to other souls in need of affection. You may remember, there was a saying in that confused and misguided decade: "No one will be denied a glass of water or a lay." The important thing, according to my parents, was to remain loyal by making each other participants in every extramarital encounter by dint of detailed accounts of each one. Say what they will, I'm convinced this practice ultimately created the rift between them.

Shortly after being bombarded with information about sex and its vicissitudes, a more contentious—and, from my point of view, also more anguishing—issue crept into our daily life. Using the recent divorce of a classmate's parents as pretext, they introduced a new book into our bedtime reading routine that used illustrations to explain how one family can have two homes. Bit by bit, my capacity for deductive reasoning led me to realize their emphasis on the topic meant it was happening to us. Despite all their faults, I appreciate that at least my parents had the tact to never fight in front of us. I have no idea how bloody and insidious their arguments grew. What I can say is that they were always cordial and restrained when my brother and I were around, and a lifetime will never be enough time to thank them for it. Maybe that's why the announcement came as something so incomprehensible to us, and so painful. For as many books as they placed in my hands, and for all the antecedent explanations, it still took me nearly a decade to understand that they were going to live apart indefinitely. One morning in late June—summer vacation had already begun—a man who worked for my dad showed up at the house under orders to take all of his books, records, and clothing from the apartment. I picked up the phone, I remember, and I called my dad to find out if these strange instructions really did come from him. I didn't interpret what was happening as the obvious act of cowardice it was, nor did I imagine how difficult it would have been for my dad to come himself. Instead, I thought that collecting his belongings from the house mattered so little to him that he'd assigned someone else the task.

That was how my father moved out of the apartment forever. They had explained it to us many times, but still, in order to fully grasp it, I needed to find myself in front of an empty bookcase in the living room. A bookshelf where for my whole life there had been records: *zarzuela*, opera, jazz, The Beatles, Simon & Garfunkel; a collection of every issue of *Life*; the Larousse Encyclopedia; the complete works of

Freud and Lacan, and I can't remember how many other things that impregnated the house with my father's eclectic and charming personality. During all the preparatory conversations I had worn the mask of the understanding daughter who reasons instead of reacts, and who would cut off a finger before aggravating her already aggravated parents. Why did I do it, Doctor? Explain it to me. What stupid reason stopped me from expressing the outrage the situation deserved? Why didn't I tell them what I was really feeling? Why didn't I threaten to commit suicide or to stop eating if they went through with the separation? Don't you see—there in my defeatism, in my complacency—a foreboding of all my present pathologies? Maybe if I'd behaved accordingly I would have been able to intervene in their decision to break up our family, and above all we could have avoided the disaster that was about to crash down on us, which no one saw coming.

The same day he sent his employee to collect his things, Dad signed a lease on a two-story, three-bedroom house with a little garden in an affluent neighborhood in the south part of the city. Even though he quickly bought new furniture and installed air-conditioning, the house never became a home. It was a temporary refuge where he wasn't going to be staying long. That's how it felt to me, anyway.

What can I say about my father? First of all, he is one of the most generous people I have ever met. And even though he had an explosive and sometimes terrifying temper, he would always quickly come back to his enthusiastic self and peculiar sense of humor. He knew by heart so many stories from *The Thousand and One Nights*, Herodotus, and the

Bible. He used to sing us songs like Julio Jaramillo's "Bodas negras" ("Black Weddings"), about a man who digs up his dead beloved's body so he can marry her, "Dónde está mi saxofón" ("Where is My Saxophone"), and "Gori Gori, muerto" ("Ding Dong Dead"). He sang in ways that made me and my brother laugh so hard we cried. The way he told them, the most hair-raising tales became hilarious. Many of the trips I took as a child, I took with my father, first in search of ophthalmologists, then later in search of some serenity in our emotionally turbulent lives. I have several boxes of photographs of my brother, my father, and me on the beach at the Pacific Ocean and Mexican Caribbean. There are also photos of one unforgettable week in Cuba.

Once our family was torn apart, the world split in two. I began to realize that my mother and father had very different ways of looking at life, more than I had imagined. My brother and I would spend a week and a half in my mother's hemisphere, in which stoicism and austerity were virtues of the highest order. In that part of the world, food absolutely had to be as nutritious as possible, even if it meant flavor was sacrificed. I remember the liver and onions we had to eat a few times a week and the infallible Hauser broth that was prepared every third day. It was a soup of fresh and root vegetables, just barely steamed in order to preserve their vitamins and minerals, but to tell you the truth, what I remember most is the utter lack of taste and those bland colored little cubes floating in the unsalted, unseasoned water. It's not that Mom didn't know how to cook; it's just that she enjoyed instilling in us a Spartan lifestyle. Another characteristic of the maternal territory was the conviction that money was an asset that could run out at any moment, and so guarding it at any cost was imperative. She couldn't stand how my father left big tips and bought expensive presents for his nieces on their fifteenth birthdays. She thought it endangered our education. She lived in constant fear of what we could become in those moments when we escaped her supervision, even for a little while. She was convinced that, if deprived of her severe vigilance, the whole world would irreparably collapse. Life was a place full of vices, ill-intentioned people, and reproachable attitudes, into the claws of which it was all too easy to fall if one lacked her courage and temperament. I'm convinced that she didn't study law out of any professional calling, as many claim, but out of an irrepressible fear of being swindled. How well I remember the February afternoon in 1984, when we got home from school and she announced, her face pale, that the peso had devalued 400 percent and most of her savings had all but evaporated. It was then she delivered one of her lectures, famous in the story of our relationship:

"Children, listen closely," she said from the head of our cedar dining table. "The world you are going to inherit when you grow up is going to be a lot tougher and harder than the world your father and I were raised in. That's why you're going to have to study and get ready to face it. Until then, you can count on me to guide you toward a future safe from harm."

What Mom really meant is that she was not going to leave us alone for one second until we had earned a university degree, a PhD at least, and had found a stable job that would allow us to scrimp and save our lives away like she was doing. Dr. Sazlavski, despite how she could come off, my mother was also an incredibly caring person, partly because it was in her nature, but also because she wanted to raise sensitive human beings who were capable of giving and receiving affection. I know that everyone sees their mother as a beautiful woman, but I can honestly say—and there is no one who would dare contradict me—that Mom surpassed all standards of beauty, and not just Mexican standards, but those of any country. She didn't read books on education—probably thinking that no one could teach her about that—but she did religiously read Wilhelm Reich and his theory of the orgasm as a cure-all elixir. While my brother and I were building sandcastles on beaches with our father, Mom was in Santa Barbara attending seminars on how to unblock her sexual energy, when what she really needed was a workshop on how to contain it. My mother was determined to cast off all her inhibitions and to keep us from ever developing our own. So she organized recreational activities at home, such as having us move our bodies to the beat of the music, or sculpt with clay then smear the same clay on our naked bodies. Watching us in action for about fifteen minutes was enough for her to see that, at least in my case, her efforts were in vain, if not counterproductive. But I never stopped writing. My general predilection was still for fantasy, with an inclination toward gore and terror, though I would also compose a poem or elegy for a flitting bird or dead plant. Unlike other grownups, who saw in this a harmless childish fancy, as eccentric as it was passing, my mother made a big fuss. She celebrated every text as a masterpiece and swore that within those paragraphs of cursive lettering and unintentionally simplistic drawings hid the signs of a strong calling. Often, and above all in the moments of my life when I feel imprisoned by my obsession for language, for constructing a plot, and for, the most absurd thing of all, turning writing into a profession, a *modus vivendi*, I blame her excessive enthusiasm. Who knows, maybe I would be happier today if every month I collected a fat paycheck from IBM.

After their separation, my mother started to hang out with a very different group of friends, artists of every kind, most of them theater people, and among them foreigners and flaming homosexuals who to me were the most fun people in the whole world. They often threw parties at night that we were never allowed to attend, but I fondly remember a few dinners and days spent in the countryside at some of their houses. Italians, Swiss, children of eminent members of the Spanish Republic in exile—all partook with us in the bacchanalia. I remember best of all Rafael Segovia, whom I saw again years later in Montreal, and Daniel Catán. Very few of them had kids. They also held dinners at our country house. Mom felt no qualms about showing my writing to her literary friends without asking my permission, and moved by god knows what sort of emotion, they responded with admiration and kindness. It can even be said that they, along with my classmates, initiated my addiction to praise, from which one may somewhat recover but never be cured.

Even though my mother's character was much gentler than that of my father, when she did lose it, she could turn violent, and then she'd hit, slap, and pull hair—delivering what could have been called *sanjuanizas*, for which she rarely apologized. Instead of admitting to having lost control, her tactic was to say we'd provoked her. It's worth noting that I was much more often the target of this kind of reprimand than my brother. And still, if in that time I had been asked if I wanted to go live with my father, Doctor, I would have flat-out said no. Call it Stockholm syndrome or whatever you think fits. My mother's house was where I had always lived, and the place I considered my own. The tree I climbed to release adrenaline after every terrifying outburst was there. Woven into those memories of her hitting me are those of her hugging me at bedtime, of her hands rubbing alcohol onto the bottoms of my feet during feverish nights, of her tender words.

Everything was the opposite on my father's continent. Austerity and stoicism became the most pointless and masochistic values in the world. My father, who in those days owned an insurance company and several garages, was a big fan of casinos, sports cars (he had an MG convertible, crimson), and the luxury of grand hotels. All it took to get him to buy us a new toy was to be in the right place and to announce that we wanted it. It didn't matter how much it cost, nor did it matter how much he had spent to indulge us the month before. I'm not going to say the events of his life haven't changed him a great deal, but back then he had the arrogance of a self-made man who'd done well in business. If that success wasn't enough, he had also mustered the tenacity, sensitivity, and intelligence to become a psychoanalyst of considerable renown (at least in the school he'd trained in), which invested his self-satisfaction with an intellectual aura. When we were with him, we were free to use swear words as we pleased—something our mother never tolerated—and we could watch PG-13 movies and stay up past our bedtime. On the other hand, he took it badly when we fought—it was one of the things that really drove him up the wall. I don't think my brother and I judged the two continents we swung between. We adapted to both belief systems, indiscriminately and unquestioningly, the way a person adapts to the climates of two different cities while living between them.

I should say that after the separation, my parents did their best to preserve the unity of the family. We'd all eat lunch at home at least once a week, and we'd often travel together during the summer. And there were some rather long stays at the country house with both of them. This simulacrum of happiness was pretty strange. In the end, we were always left nostalgic for what we could have been and didn't get to be, but it was still better than nothing.

There weren't many vacations my brother and I took with just my mother, and of those, there is only one I remember well—to the state of Sonora. In those days, my mother was particularly interested in community living. Maybe she was thinking that since the traditional matrimonial structure hadn't worked out for her, other, newer—or more archaic—systems might lead her to a fulfilling life. So we went to Sonora to visit a commune known as Los Horcones. We flew to Hermosillo, where we rented a car and drove around the desert until we found the place. We

arrived in the evening, at dinnertime. As soon as they heard
the car motor, a few of the oldest members of the commune came out to greet us and ushered us into the dining
room, which looked like a school cafeteria and where some
sixty people sat around huge wooden tables. The food was
simple but tasted so good: frijoles charros, beef stew with
a tomato base, flour tortillas. After five hours of traveling
we were starving and ate ravenously. During dinner they
explained to us their rules of cohabitation. I'm writing
down the ones that stuck in my memory.

Rule 1: There was no private property. Objects belonged
to nobody. Not a toothbrush, not underwear, shoes, food,
or beds had owners in this place. All was *communal.*

Rule 2: Children were also communal. All the adults
were responsible for taking care of every child as if they
were their own.

Rule 3: Everyone had a farm chore. The young kids were
in charge of milking the cows.

The purpose of this vacation, my mother explained to
us, was to see if we could adapt to the system well enough
to be able to move there. That first night, after dinner, they
took Lucas (no longer *my* brother) and me to a huge dormitory where all the children slept, but not, of course, in
beds assigned to them. I'll admit that at first the idea was
thrilling. In my short life, every time we'd been allowed to
sleep unsupervised with more than two kids to a room, it
was guaranteed to be a fun time: pillow fights, hide-and-
seek, climbing on the drapes. We'd take full advantage of
every resource the room had to offer. This time, there were
fifteen of us and it was sure to be a party that lasted all

night. But things went a little differently than I expected. As soon as they opened the door to let us in, the other kids threw off their clothes and—without brushing their teeth or washing their faces—stampeded inside to grab the best beds. Once in a bed, there was no moving from it. Diego and Maria, two adolescents of about twelve, the oldest in the dormitory, were in charge of making sure no one was missing and turning off the light. Not one joke was heard that night in the silence, deep and rural, full of crickets and hooting owls. The kids immediately fell asleep. Lost in the pajama'd multitude, my brother must have been surprised too. I had a good idea of where his bed was, but with the lights out it was impossible to find him to talk about what was going on. Besides, I'd be risking giving someone the chance to take my spot.

Lucas and I woke up at dawn with the others and went to get the metal pails used for milking the cows. I don't think I had ever been so close to one of those animals in my life, much less to their wrinkly udders. Someone explained to us how to squeeze the udders to get the milk, then left us to the mercy of the cow, who was growing impatient in our clumsy hands. We walked out of there with a half-empty bucket and drew annoyed expressions from those in charge, but since we'd never done it before no one criticized us. They called us "the newcomers," and hearing those words made my stomach cramp, to think we could end up staying in this weird place. It all came down to a simple decision my mother would make—my mother, who was clearly at the moment a bit disoriented when it came to her life plan. After milking, we went into the dining hall, where our breakfast was almost ready, except for the milk that needed to be boiled before we could drink it. Diego, the boy who had turned off the lights the night before, sat at our table. Our life in Mexico City awakened in him a morbid curiosity. He asked us for details about our school and public transportation, and he wanted to know how the streets smelled. He had been told the capital smelled like shit and the people who lived there were the nastiest kind.

"At least everyone knows which bed is theirs," I responded, "and nobody takes it from us."

One day there was enough for me to understand the baffling behavior of the first night. A full day of working in the barn, shining shoes, scrubbing floors, and washing plates was so tiring that none of us had the strength or energy to play. After breakfast the next day, we saw our mother again. She hugged us as if nothing had changed and, forgetting the code of behavior, called us *her* treasures, *her* little pieces of heaven, as always. One of the leaders of the commune, an extremely tall and rotund man, with the same limp black hair that Yaqui Indians often have, but dressed as a Mennonite, showed a particular fondness for our mother and offered to give us a guided tour of the grounds that morning. The commune was huge. In addition to the cows, there were sheep, pigs, and chickens. They also grew vegetables using hydroponics to feed the sixty-three inhabitants. However, the true purpose of that place, and what gave it some prestige in the region and some protection from the local government, was carried out in a different building from the one we slept in. It was a kind of school for children and adolescents with Down syndrome. Some of them were

Mexican but most were American, children whose parents could not—or didn't want to—take care of them and so paid large sums of money for other people to keep them in the middle of the desert. The farmer who eyed my mother with obvious erotic appreciation explained to us that the people who were in charge of these children "with problems" had received their training in Mexican schools and in San Antonio, Texas. We stopped to watch the children from the edge of the garden during one of their recesses. They looked happy and friendly, much more so than the kids we'd spent the night with. When I saw them running around on the grass, dying of laughter, hugging each other and caressing each other's hair, I told myself that if anyone had problems here it wasn't these kids but everyone else. It was the first time I'd encountered the segregation of "different" people, or people with, as it is said even today, some kind of "disability." I also told myself that if I had been born in this commune, maybe I would have been placed in a separate house, far from the other kids, the "normal" ones who worked liked beasts to be accepted, those kids who ever since I arrived at the farm had not stopped asking what had happened to my eye—why was there a dense storm cloud in the middle of it? Deep down I felt sorry for those children because I knew, sooner or later, that my mother would come to her senses and take us home.

The heat and very different living conditions made it feel like an eternity, but I know we didn't stay long at the commune. On the third day, an enraged woman, probably involved with the Yaqui farmer, confronted my mother in the middle of breakfast and accused her of stealing *her* man.

Apparently children didn't belong to anyone but fathers did. The woman looked so upset and violent that no one, not even the Yaqui, dared to intervene. When she screamed that we should go back to the "urban sewer we came from," my mother rose from the table and took us to the car. As the car turned onto the highway that crossed the desert, I thanked the Sonoran heavens above for delivering us from communal living and returning us to the jungle—savage, sure, but at least familiar—of capitalism.

I saw Diego again, the older kid who oversaw the children's dormitory, almost twenty years later in Puerto Vallarta. I was there participating in a literary festival. He was on vacation with his family, at the same hotel. As strange as it may seem, we immediately recognized each other. I was eating breakfast alone on the hotel terrace, so he invited me to join and asked if I remembered his wife. I said I didn't.

"You have no idea," he said, "how much your visit changed our lives. To see you with your mother and your brother, to hear about life outside, it made us so jealous, and made us think about the possibility of leaving someday."

"They shut down the commune?" I asked. "Or were you a special case?"

"Patricia and I left. And now here we are, enjoying this luxury hotel we never could have imagined as children."

He was talking about his wife, who was sitting with us, and he continued speaking for her and their family all morning. He hadn't lost his Sonoran accent. Diego and Patricia had left Los Horcones six years ago. Since then, they had procreated four times. I looked over at their children running around the pool. I thought, after a childhood like theirs, it must have been that neither one of them could adjust to life alone.

Two years after separating from my father, Mom fell into a deep depression that ultimately affected us all. Her pain manifested as a recurring wailing that would burst out and drown the afternoon, like the summer downpours in Mexico City. Every afternoon she locked herself in her room for several hours to cry, sometimes very loudly. It had to do in part with unrequited love. Loyal to her custom of not keeping anything from us, Mom had explained that she'd had an affair with a married man who had broken many promises to her. Despite her otherwise rational and practical nature, she started consulting the *I Ching* several times a week, which she herself deemed unhealthy and reprehensible. Also during that time, she took to interpreting the results of some medical tests with determined pessimism. One Saturday morning she called us into her room to announce that her health was in danger. I can still see her lying in her unmade bed, with the drawn curtains creating an atmosphere of artificial darkness. "They're doing tests," she told us. "It doesn't look good, I may be very sick."

"What if I die?" she said.

She didn't tell us what the possible diagnoses were. Of course we hugged her and told her she wasn't going to die and that we were going to be together forever. But the agony had already taken hold of the afternoon and the week. She later calmed down and dropped the subject for a few days. But she gave us at least three false alarms. What do you think, Dr. Sazlavski, about needlessly terrifying children of that age? "Normal behavior for a disturbed woman going through a particularly hard time," you'll tell me, and you'll be right, but back then we couldn't see our mother as anything other than our family's sturdiest pillar. I remember so well the feeling of helplessness that overwhelmed me as I listened to her crying through the door. Her wailing brought every activity at home to a standstill, even my games and the maid's comings and goings. My brother and I would sit on our beds waiting for the storm to pass. We'd stay there in expectant silence until at last the tears dried and it was possible to go back to our games and evening rituals. Used to keeping a tight hold on the reins of her life, my mother fought a fierce internal struggle against all her emotions. Her strong side was fighting a losing battle. At least that's how it was for nearly three years, during which time she placed herself in the hands of the most useless psychoanalyst I've ever heard of.

Finally, in a burst of desperate willpower, she decided to exile herself. Hers was not political, but an exile of love. The pretext was getting a doctorate in urban and regional planning in the south of France. My parents agreed that for the first year of her program we would live with my father in Mexico while my mother got things ready for us to move overseas. Lucas and I would study French during that time. That's not how it went, however. Something happened in Dad's life that kept us from going through with the plan— something we would find out about almost a year later, when it would come as a blow and turn our lives upside down. One of the first signs of this new situation was that my father started coming by the house less and less. When we asked about him, we were told he was on a trip dealing with some stuff that had to do with his business in San Diego. After three months of bureaucratic procedures, the French government gave my mother a grant that let her vanish. Which she did, in mid-July. As decided, we stayed in Mexico, in the same apartment where we had always lived. But instead of my father, the person who came to look after us was our maternal grandmother. That, Dr. Sazlavski, turned out to be the most grim and confusing period of my entire life. Why the hell our father stayed out of the country was something no one could tell us. What could have been so important to keep him from being with us when we needed him the most? Why would my mother seize this opportunity to travel even though it meant leaving us in the hands of her aged and conservative mother, whose ideas embodied exactly the kind of upbringing she *didn't* want to give us? Why, after preaching the importance of always telling the truth, did no one give us a convincing explanation? The only person there for me to ask was my grandmother herself. Her answer was cryptic and always the same: "Since when do ducks shoot rifles?" she'd say, meaning that children should not demand accountability from adults.

II.

While the two parental hemispheres never gave me and my brother any navigational problems, the nineteenth-century grandmother universe was the least hospitable territory we'd known. This universe was governed, at least in my opinion, by completely arbitrary laws that took me months to assimilate. Many of them were based on the supposed inferiority of women. The way my grandmother saw it, a little girl's duty, first and foremost—even before going to school—was to help clean the home. Furthermore, ladies were supposed to dress and behave "appropriately," whereas men could do whatever they pleased. So it was that I, a fan of the jeans and athletic pants that let me comfortably climb stone walls, had to go back several decades in fashion evolution to incorporate into my everyday outfits lacey dresses and patent-leather shoes. This, in the middle of the eighties, the decade my grandmother hadn't noticed we were in. A real blow to anyone's dignity. Little girls were not supposed to run around in the street loosey-goosey and play with boys, and they certainly were not

supposed to climb trees. That we should question her deci-
sions—something our teachers and parents had taught us
to do—showed in my grandmother's eyes a lack of respect
and a dangerous demonstration of insolence that needed to
be repressed, swiftly and mercilessly. On top of all her general prejudices, my grandmother was constantly criticizing
the way I walked and how I moved. She made my mother's
corrective agenda look like child's play. Though she never
said an offensive word about my limited eyesight, she constantly criticized the ungainly posture that my mother had
so viciously attacked early on. According to her, there was a
hump forming in my back that looked more like a camel's
than a cockroach's.

"For the love of God, stand up straight!" she'd command
ten times a day at least, her voice shaking the walls of the
apartment. She even gave me a back brace, which disappeared into the farthest corner of my closet. She called
my curly hair (very similar to hers at my age, by the way)
unkempt whenever I didn't wear it straightened and tied
back. Even the way I spoke was something she constantly
criticized. She accused me for no reason of pronouncing
my *s*'s like a Colombian and demanded that I practice
keeping my tongue away from my teeth to avoid whistling.
I didn't do it, obviously.

Unlike me, who got on her nerves constantly, my
brother received my grandmother's evident adoration. She
endlessly extolled his virtues and, when speaking to other
members of the family, told them all how wonderful her
grandson was and how his mere presence brought her such
joy. I remember once, at the very beginning of her stay at

our house, my brother asked if we could go down to the garden where every afternoon there were soccer matches between the kids in the unit. She said it was fine, and so we went and stayed out until dark. We came home, our clothing caked with mud and our knees all scraped up, to find our grandmother in a state of alarm. According to her, she'd gone down several times to find us, and as we were nowhere in sight, she was about to call LOCATEL, the service for finding people who are missing, in hospital, or dead. She said nothing about the condition of my brother's knees; she went off about mine as if they were proof of my indecency.

"It looks like you've been rolling around in the dirt," she claimed indignantly. By that time, I'd already figured out how to decipher the moral implications of her commentaries.

My grandmother's techniques of repression were unlike any of those I had known before. The punishments my parents dolled out were clear and to the point: locking us in our rooms for an hour "to think about what we'd done," or, when the crime was particularly serious or infuriating, a series of "well-placed spanks" (a phrase they often used to justify the use of corporal punishment or a humiliating beating). But our grandmother relied on torture methods much more subtle and disturbing. Among them was the so-called silent-treatment, in which she pretended that the person who had done wrong did not exist, and therefore could not be heard nor spoken to. After that soccer match, my grandmother lovingly bathed my brother. She also cooked him dinner, tucked him into bed, and stayed

with him until he fell asleep. I, on the other hand, was
sent to bed on an empty stomach, because there was no
food for invisible beings. Rather than display a more sub-
missive attitude, I decided on resistance. My mission—an
idiotic assignment that I'd taken on without realizing it
and that I have maintained throughout almost my entire
life—was to not let anything or anyone make me cry, no
matter what. It was a pleasure I was not about to grant my
grandmother, nor anyone else. But how badly I needed to
cry in that moment! And who can say? Maybe if I'd been
able to move my grandmother, she would have changed
the way she treated me. Instead, I became determined to
defy her as much as I could. I had always been thought of
as the antisocial one in the building, but I started going
out every afternoon. I didn't hang out with the sixth-grade
girls who played jacks or jump rope next to the parking lot,
or with the ones who demurely repeated their multiplication tables ad nauseum behind the bushes. I hung out with
the boys who played soccer. What my body needed was
to take all that rage mounting inside and expel it through
physical activity. The rage toward my mother, who called
once in a while from a faraway country. The rage toward
my father, who had vanished from the face of the earth
without a word. The rage toward this unfair old woman
who tried everything in her power to puncture my inflated
ego, as if the circumstances of my life hadn't already and
with great success taken on that task. Luckily, the boys
from my building didn't mind my joining the matches, as
long as I kept the other team from scoring; because of my
height—I was taller than all of them—they had me play

defense. True, it wasn't easy going home after the games, but I much preferred my grandmother's lengthy chastisements to spending entire afternoons under her thumb.

I should say, Dr. Sazlavski, that to me my grandmother was more than just a simple interrogator with backward thinking. She was also one of the most original people I've ever had the chance to live with. She was full of manias and strange habits, some of which I was picking up without realizing it. She'd left her house in a central neighborhood to come live with us. Her house, which she visited every day, was a warehouse of everything imaginable. A victim of what is commonly referred to as Diogenes syndrome, my grandmother saved piles of journals and copies of the newspaper *Excélsior* from the forties. Her beloved and disorderly archive took up two bedrooms. In addition to these papers, in her closet she kept not only the clothing of her deceased husband, but also her own old clothes and things, and those of her children from over three decades. This tidal wave of anachronistic objects— shoes, pocketbooks, wedding gowns, stuffed animals, fancy hats, transistor radios, gloves, globes, books, combs, jewelry boxes, dolls, and who knows what else—formed a kind of living mass that ebbed and flowed as the house needed it to. We called it "the green wave." If one of her daughters who had settled down in the provinces decided to spend the summer in Mexico City, my grandmother would empty the central bedrooms and send the wave to the basement and garage. This took days, sometimes weeks, of grueling labor. Even though there were many different smells mixing in that place, the most potent was mothballs. She said herself that during her pregnancies she developed an intense liking for those poisonous little moth-banishing balls. She took to sucking on them like hard candies. It was impressive how, despite the contained disorder, the house was able to maintain its dignity and elegance. The furniture was almost all antique but in excellent condition. The parquet floors were covered in carpets brought over from Iran. My grandfather had dedicated his final years to traveling the entire world for months at a time with his wife. Many of the objects bought on those trips adorned the house. There were bronze lamps, menorahs, and marble statues in display cases and on coffee tables. All those trinkets and, above all, the Japanese pottery with its motifs drawn in a very faint blue, ignited my imagination and helped save me from an otherwise nearly unbearable reality. The house continued to be occupied by a servant who, in the absence of the lady of the house, turned her efforts on her own personal improvement. Our grandmother preferred her to stay there than to come live with us and leave the house vulnerable to robberies. Even though our grandmother almost always used public transportation, she kept a brand new car in the garage, a white Celebrity with leather seats, and whenever it was needed she hired a chauffer to drive her where she wanted to go.

There are some kinds of fungi that can travel several miles on near-invisible, food-detecting feet. In a similar manner, the reach of "the wave" extended beyond the limits of the house. After the arrival of our grandmother, the rooms of our apartment started to fill with clothing and paper waiting to one day be classified. Only, no matter what, the disorder was not permitted to reach the top of the bed she obsessively made every morning, smoothing out even the smallest wrinkle in the sheets and quilt. But it did infiltrate her relationship to time, such that she was late for everything, including picking us up from school. Ever since she'd come, meal times ceased to be respected. For her, with her stomach smaller than a prune, eating three spoonfuls of rice was enough fuel to live on, and she insisted that we growing children eat the same. She never liked to cook and probably had never learned how. Often she bought a plain pizza base consisting of dough and tomato from the frozen foods section of the grocery and served it to us at three-thirty in the afternoon, without toppings or side dishes. Even though her menus were unworthy, at every meal she enforced the use of the table manners that her favorite writer, Antonio Carreño, preached. In the months we were under her care, I heard her speak of his manual several times a day, but it was years before I came face-to-face with an actual copy. At a book fair I went to as a literature student, I discovered the dusty volume of over a hundred pages whose complete title was: *Manual of Urbanity and Good Manners for Youths of Both Sexes in Which is Found the Principles of Civility and Etiquette that One Must Observe in Diverse Social Situations, Preceded by a Brief Treatise on the Moral Obligations of Man*. I bought it out of masochistic nostalgia. It proved to be a very practical and illustrative read, explaining, for example, how a woman is to step down from a carriage that is pulled by one or more horses.

Inconspicuously, my brother and I got into the habit of

inviting ourselves to eat at the house of another member of the soccer team—a different one each time—which no doubt made things very easy for our grandmother. The kids of Villa Olímpica—that is, the kids of our generation, the ones we knew and with whom we played in the afternoons— all had a double personality, or at least a double culture. In the gardens and plaza they spoke with Mexican accents and expressions, but as soon as they got home they spoke with their parents in pristine Buenos Aires Argentinean or Santiago Chilean. Many of those kids didn't seem to be aware of the horror their families had known before leaving their birth cities. Others were tormented by memories of separation and grief—of violence and god knows what else—so much so that despite our young age it was impossible not to see it. Among them was Ximena, about whom I will say more later, the only girl I came to identify with in those days and who, perhaps without ever knowing it, left a profound impression on my story.

It took me years to pick a soccer team I wanted to root for. I felt no affinity for any of those I had watched play in the first division tournaments. Finally, when I had to choose, I opted for the Unión de Curtidores, the least glamorous team, the most obscure, and the least likely to ever win a championship. Let me tell you, Doctor, about this team that you will probably never hear of again in your life. Most people think it's a team of losers, and nobody can believe that I would seriously support such a scruffy squad. I'm not just talking about the white jersey with its diagonal dark blue stripe reminiscent of Miss Universe's sash, but also about how fatalistically they played. The only thing special about them was their nervous back-and-forth between first and second division. It was a team that lived always on the edge of tragedy, on the edge of disgrace, in the darkest of uncertainties. Their goal was not to win a championship—they didn't dream of it—but to maintain their composure. On a smaller scale, they epitomized our national team, which every four years anxiously wondered if they would make it to the World Cup. I've never been able to understand why so many Mexicans are for Club América and its multimillionaire owner, and not for the Unión de Curtidores, which truly represent us. I guess it's for reasons similar to why, presidential election after presidential election, the lower classes vote for the right-wing Catholic candidate. Despite what people think, the Unión never disappeared. The team has changed its name over the years, but its essence remains the same. Like the oldest animals that roam the earth, the Curtidores have had to mutate to survive.

Sometimes our grandmother was moved to buy chocolates or some other sweet and to distribute this wealth, which is to say that she would hide it somewhere in her closet in order to control the moment and manner in which we might eat it. One afternoon while searching for my hair tie, I peered into the space between the floor and the base of her bed, not really aware of what I was doing, and I discovered one of her best hiding places. There I found an entire bag of lychees, now completely fermented, which she had brought to the house three weeks before. There was also a cookie box full of old family photos and a pack of Belgian chocolates that, despite their still-edible appearance, I didn't dare try. Another one of my grandmother's habits was to write down in lined, hardcover notebooks every event of the day, no matter how trivial, and every object or food item she'd bought, for herself or the house, and to include the weight or quantity. According to how she herself explained it to me, she'd done this since the first day of her wedded life in 1935, so that my grandfather could never accuse her of squandering money. And she continued doing it, eleven years after his death, because of inertia or motives nobody has been able to assess. She taught me that an obsessive personality is not always someone with clean fingernails and impeccably kept hair, or one whose house looks like a window display, but a tense soul who is perpetually afraid of chaos taking complete control of her life and the lives of her loved ones.

My grandmother didn't like to be touched more than was strictly necessary. She wasn't against giving kisses, but only bestowed them if there was a compelling reason to do so. In the entire time she lived with us, she gave me two. I'll tell you later, Doctor, about those occasions. The problem with having parents as affectionate as mine is that later, once they were gone, I desperately missed the physical contact, which neither my grandmother nor anyone else could give me in those days. To make matters worse, my mother called from France only a few times a month and, because of the time difference, almost never when we were home. Grandmother would tell us—who knows if it was true—that she had chatted with her, that our mother had sent her love and that, even though she missed us very much, "she was enjoying herself." As selfish as it sounds, knowing that my mother was happy in some faraway part of the world did not make me feel the same. Of course it was good to hear that over there, on the other side of the Atlantic, she wasn't crying every day, but between that and "she was enjoying herself" stood an abyss. More than once, suffocated by the feeling of unfairness that permeated our home, I would have done anything to be able to contact her, to speak with her for a long time and tell her what I was going through. But it was never possible. Long distance calls in those days were very uncommon. Anyway, I didn't have a number to call, and this made me feel utterly abandoned.

Around that time, something very strange started happening. One Saturday at about eleven o'clock, while we were getting ready to go to a family lunch in a different part of the city, and after an intense discussion about the clothing I was to wear that day, I found a caterpillar in my shoe. A hairy caterpillar of a light, bright green. I tried to get it out by smacking the shoe's heel against the floor a few times, but the caterpillar didn't seem to mind. Aided by its suction-cup feet, it comfortably withstood the blows.

"Hurry up we're already late!" thundered the voice of my grandmother, abruptly breaking the trance I found myself in. And so I decided to put on different shoes and went back to getting ready to go. Just as I was at the door, my grandmother asked me why I was wearing those chunky shoes and not the white ballerina flats with the straps that she had bought me. So I told her what had happened. As might be expected, she didn't believe me for a second and set off exasperated in search of the shoes and, when she had retrieved them, the caterpillar was no longer inside. What had been the poor creature's fate? I didn't dare ask. Once we were at lunch, I began to feel something moving just under the sole of my foot. The sensation was so disturbing that I was forced to crawl under the table to confirm what I already feared. I again saw the caterpillar, injured from the weight of my body and oozing a dark liquid over my brand new sock. Finding it there all over again, now with its body mangled, provoked in me an incontrollable fear and I began to scream hysterically. I don't know if my grandmother didn't see the bug that time, or if she just didn't want to admit she'd been wrong. The point is that she grabbed my arm, pulled me out from under the table where everyone was eating, and locked me in a separate room—exactly how one might throw an undesirable insect outside so as to not have to squash it in front of guests. From that room, I listened to her complain about my temperament, and I also heard the unflattering comments several family members made about my mother and me. Poor grandmother, they said, we were making the final years of her life—which until then had passed so pleasantly—so very unpleasant. Later that night, when we went home and it was at last time to go to bed, I saw the caterpillar again, in my sheets. It was then that I too began to doubt my sanity.

Insects continued to show up in my bedroom frequently. And not only caterpillars but other, often poisonous critters came to visit. It might have been a red spider, a praying mantis, a potato bug, but never a butterfly nor cricket, only much rarer bugs that would appear suddenly and make me scream. It wasn't the threat of the insects that filled me with panic, nor that everyone accused me of lying to get attention. What made me react the way I did was the possibility that I—and at such a young age—might have an important screw loose. If I couldn't count on myself, who could I count on? If the truth was something inaccessible to me, how could I accept other people's versions of it—those who branded me a liar, insolent, and churlish little-old-lady killer? In the presence of the insects and all those unanswered questions, the only thing I could think to do was stop thinking as much as possible and play, play, play soccer and, during breaks, to talk about it, until falling into bed dead from exhaustion, even if it meant missing dinner. The night I saw the resuscitated caterpillar in the sheets, it felt like something inside me had changed. Something very deep and inaccessible had altered within my consciousness. I couldn't go back to bed. Neither could I seek refuge with someone in the house, so I sat up in front of my bedroom window and there I stayed awake for several hours. Night is rarely a land that belongs to children. I'd slept well my entire life and I wasn't one of those people who linger listening to the noises of the early hours. To take my thoughts off the bug, I went and found my binoculars and focused my mind—normally poured into reverie and fantastical tales—on what was going on below the building. Standing there, through the curtains, I watched men in suits looking drunk and tired park their cars then walk to their doors; I watched a teenager and his girlfriend appear and disappear several times behind the bushes in front of the parking lot; I watched a cat skirting traffic in a suicide game. Nothing captured my interest for very long until I raised my gaze and discovered that in the facing building, at the same height as our apartment, in a marvelous symmetry, there was another girl observing the world from her window with a face as unhappy as mine must have been. Her name was Ximena. I knew her by sight, and I liked her. On various occasions, I had watched her crossing the street with that somewhat absent look of hers. But I can say, this night I saw her for the first time, not indifferently as one often observes the comings and goings of a neighbor, but truly mindfully, and empathetically. I couldn't be sure, but something made me feel that she was also watching me. All of the sudden the distance separating our buildings became very small and I felt that, if I tried, I could have seen her breath printed in steam on the window, and I could have heard her breathing and known what she was going through.

That night marked the beginning of a tradition: when the lights in each of our apartments went out, she and I would have our meeting. The ritual was to stand facing each other, and thus to keep the other company until sleep overcame us. We never communicated through any orthodox means, neither there nor anywhere else, but, consciously or unconsciously, Ximena made me feel that despite my parents' absence, and my absolute uncertainty about what was to come, I had someone in this world I could count on. Think what you want, Dr. Sazlavski, I'm convinced—and now, more than ever—that this communication happened and was so profound that it surpassed spatial and temporal limits, as often occurs between the closest people. What I knew about her wasn't a lot, but it was enough to give me some idea of her emotions. I knew, as I mentioned before, that she was Chilean and had lived in that building with her mother and sister since coming to Mexico. Pinochet's men had riddled her father with bullets before he could get out of Santiago. In contrast to Paula, her younger sister, who was blond with light-eyes and a light-hearted nature, Ximena was taciturn. Her hair and expression were dark and so too were her thoughts, probably. Maybe she was thinking nostalgically about the days peace reigned in her country, about her family and all the happy memories she stored in her soul. She almost never went out to the plaza, and when she did it wasn't to join in the games with the other kids. She liked to sit under the tree near the parking lot, same as me, but instead of climbing the branches, she remained with the stones and roots. Ximena did oil paintings. I had seen her a few times staring at her easel in that bedroom half revealed to me through the limited reach of my binoculars. What was her relationship with her family like? What school did she go to and how did she get along with her classmates? These and a dozen other questions struck me at night as I watched her from my room. I also liked to find similarities between us, beyond the placement of our windows, like the color of our hair and the fact that childhood was not a bed of roses for either one of us.

One afternoon when I was particularly sad and in urgent need of meeting Ximena, I appeared at the window before it was time, to see if by chance I could get a glimpse of her through her bedroom curtains, even just a fleeting one.

I saw there was a fire in her apartment. I flung open my bedroom door and shouted to my grandmother to call the fire department. I remember that I went running into the street and up onto the mound with the tree and waited for the firemen to arrive. It was then I realized: the image was not a picture of normal burning with fire coming out of the windows, but a much more subtle spectacle. The flames formed a silhouette like a tree of light. After an unbearably long time, we heard the sirens and, with them, we saw the fire truck appear. An ambulance also came to take Ximena out on a stretcher. We later found out, from some neighbors in her building, that she had bathed in oil paint solvent and started a fire in her bedroom. The news was in all the papers. Someone uttered the word "schizophrenic." For me, the explanation was simple: Ximena had resolved to escape once and for all the cage of her life.

Never again would she keep me company from her bedroom. But the coincidences did not end with her death. Many years later, after my first books were published, I was invited to join a panel of judges for a short story contest the Chilean journal *Paula* organizes every year. I visited Santiago on a whirlwind trip filled with activities. Traveling the streets of this city, I thought of some of the kids who had shared part of my childhood. Had they returned to their countries with the arrival of democracy? And, if so, would they recognize themselves in these renovated and shiny streets, where years earlier their families had been persecuted? I thought of Ximena, of course, and also of a few others with tragic stories like Javiera Enríquez, whom I met later as a teenager, and who had lost her family when she was four years old. The one morning I had off, I asked to visit Pablo Neruda's home in Isla Negra, an hour from the capital. Along with my ten-month-old son, I was accompanied by Silvia Ossandón, an editor from the magazine, whom I had become friends with. We were met by the person in charge of public relations for la Casa Neruda, a man who had lived in exile in Mexico and who immediately took a liking to me. His name was Bernardo Baltiansky. We spoke a little bit before my tour through the museum house. We discovered that in the eighties we had lived in the same neighborhood. As I looked at the innumerable collections of the late author of *I Confess I Have Lived*, at all the remnants of his time on earth, I had only one thing on my mind, Ximena. When I left I was going to ask this man if he had known her, if he could tell me something about her—any piece of information, any fact that would bring me closer to her would satisfy me. I needed to find a way to bring up the subject. While thinking about it, Bernardo told me that in his lifetime Neruda had written, traveled, carried out diplomatic duties, been married several times, and above all had built houses and furniture, a colossal oeuvre. Ximena in turn had passed through the world on feet unsure and slippery. Her time here had been short, but resplendent for those of us lucky enough to have seen her.

At the end of the tour, Bernardo invited us to have a drink in the museum café. The ocean waves lapped the sand a few meters away. It seemed like the water's smooth persistence whispered secrets from the not too distant past when Chile's coast had seen the most terrible atrocities, secrets no one was ready to hear, as if what those people most feared was waking the ghosts of the disappeared. Silvia reminded me that if we wanted to find an open restaurant we should leave soon. I asked Bernardo if he had known other Chileans in Villa Olímpica. As if he had expected the question, he answered yes, his sister had also lived there with her daughters.

"My niece committed suicide in one of those buildings," he said.

Inside my body, I felt my blood turn as cold as the waves of the cobalt sea.

"What was her name?" I asked, knowing it could be no one else. Bernardo confirmed it. He also told me that some months before her death his niece had been diagnosed with schizophrenia, an illness that served to encompass all the unclassifiable disorders, and which also happened to be the diagnosis for Javiera Enríquez. Bernardo spoke of her without telling me anything I didn't already know. Until he started talking about her painting.

"She was very talented. The best painting she did is still in my sister's house. It's of an immense tree that grew in Villa Olímpica, just in front of her house, where she spent many hours."

"And your sister?" I asked, "does she still live there?"

"No, she lives in Santiago. If you'd like, we can call her."

That evening I had promised to have dinner at my writer friend Alejandro Zambra's house. When I got there, I told him the story and asked him to go with me to the woman's apartment. It wasn't far from where he lived and he readily agreed. As soon as Ximena's mother opened the door, I saw the painting on the main wall of her living room. It had a power of attraction, like a face with a strong magnetism. At least that's the effect it had on me. It really was a portrait of our tree, if trees can belong to people. On the volcanic rocks there were silhouettes of children sitting in front of one another and back-to-back, children whose faces couldn't clearly be made out, pensive children who played neither together nor alone. Children like we had been. The painting moved me to tears. All of a sudden, that feeling of abandonment, a constant in those years, came back to life; but so too did the composure I had always maintained, in those days when letting others see me cry was the last thing I'd do. Habits we develop in childhood stay with us forever, and even though we are able by force of great will to keep them at bay, crouching in a sinister place in our memory, when we least expect them they leap into our faces like enraged cats. I focused on the other paintings Ximena's mother was showing me and politely answered the questions she asked. It wasn't a long conversation. I believe that neither of us was ready to open the floodgate of emotions for the fear of the torrents that would wash over us; our feelings were only exposed at their tips like icebergs moving beneath the surface. Even though it was my day off, I was on a work trip and didn't want to enter into the vulnerable space that encroaches every time I invoke with words all those memories, a space from which it takes me several days to climb out. Nor did I want to hurt her or to put her in a similar state. In that house, Alejandro and I drank tea, spoke about literature, and let my son play with a Moroccan drum. I found out that Paula, her other daughter, had also returned to Santiago, had become a mother like me, and was a fan of Manu Chao. Then we left, leaving behind no trace but a forgotten pacifier.

After Ximena's death, the presence of insects became much more frequent and commonplace, but no longer scared me. I had learned there were things much more terrifying than those diminutive little animals, venomous as they could be. I should also say that the insects were no longer as poisonous. Instead of burning bugs and tarantulas, I saw earthworms, beetles, and cockroaches. In my visions, the last in particular showed me friendliness, even kindness. Unlike other insects, cockroaches didn't look at me with aggressive or challenging eyes, but the opposite; they seemed to be there to keep the other critters from coming to bother me. That's why, whenever I found one in my room, instead of the usual nervousness, a mysterious calm would come over me.

Except for my grandmother's mess, the apartment remained exactly as my mother had left it. Many of her clothes were still in the closet, like the old gray robe she almost always wore at home. We called it "the skin." Her desk was the same, her pencils still sharp. Her library stood unmoved, including the *I Ching*. Everything gave the impression that she had only left for the weekend and at any moment would return to her regular life. Maybe we would have missed her less if we'd moved to a completely different place in which she had never set foot, where at least there wouldn't be a trace of her to find. During the few times I was left alone in the house, I carefully went through her belongings, as if searching for an encrypted message that could tell me the exact date of her return and give me some sign that she definitely was coming back. And that was how, looking through her books and at pieces of paper slipped between their pages, I came upon a book whose title immediately caught my attention. It was a novella by Gabriel García Márquez, *The Incredible and Sad Tale of Innocent Eréndira and Her Heartless Grandmother*. It was a Saturday morning. My grandmother had taken my brother to the mall near the house. I opened the book and began to read voraciously. Since my mother had left, I had set aside many of the things I liked to do. I didn't even slide down the service staircase to refresh my body and mind when it was hot out anymore. In those months I read very little and wrote nothing at all. Books made my grandmother suspicious. She knew that in her daughter's library there were some rather uncivilized works, such as those that explained new ways to approach sex. She didn't like to see me in the study and every time she caught me prowling the shelves she complained.

"I don't know why your mother left all those books there, where you and your brother can get to them. She should have put them away. It wouldn't be a bad idea to sell them by the pound," said the woman who stored magazines from the 1930s in the bedrooms of her house.

I didn't want my grandmother to sell my mother's books to a second-hand dealer, so even though it meant denying myself them, I preferred to pretend they didn't interest me. But the morning I found that novel I wasn't ready to give it up and I read—I read as much as I could while she was gone, and when she came back I kept reading in the bathroom and in secret under the sheets once the door to my room was closed. The pages told the story of a girl, barely older than I was, enslaved by her pimp grandmother and determined to get away. Eréndira tried everything— from shooting the old women in the head to killing her slowly with rat poison—but her grandmother survived every weapon. On top of that, the book spoke of love, politics, eroticism. In short, it was exactly the kind of book my grandmother did not want to see in my hands, and this transgression made it particularly appetizing. Doctor, this discovery, as exaggerated as it sounds, was like meeting a guardian angel, or at least a friend I could trust, which was, in those days, equally unlikely. The book understood me better than anyone in the world and, if that was not enough, made it possible for me to speak about things that were hard to admit to myself, like the undeniable urge to kill someone in my family.

This was also when I met a boy, a little older than me, who was the brother of a team member and who could make me nervous with his mere presence. His name was Oscar Soldevila and he lived in Building Six. I don't remember that much about him. I know he had longish limp hair and bangs falling over one of his eyes like a pirate. I can't say if he really was handsome or if my perception is owed to the large amount of hormones that, unbeknownst to me, were staging a revolution inside my body. It wasn't the first time I liked a boy, but it was the first time this feeling came with such a production of estrogen. While he played well, soccer wasn't Oscar's main interest. I knew that he liked to read and that, unlike me, he liked to hang out with older kids and not with his little brother's friends. It's not that I found older kids boring or uninteresting. I think it was just the opposite: I thought they were so interesting I was convinced I could never be their friend. What I remember most about Oscar is the sense of euphoria that came over me when he was close. I'm sure this feeling was mutual, at least for a while, because every time he played with us and scored a goal I was the one he hugged in celebration. And there was the afternoon we both hid in the same spot while playing hide-and-seek with the others. For a few minutes, I listened to his uneasy breathing with mine, as if he had run up all the floors in the building. I wanted something to happen but I didn't know what, exactly. And of course nothing did happen. I went home and opened my mother's *I Ching* to a random page, like she did during the height of her obsession, to find out what I could divine. I'll never forget the phrase I read that day because it described exactly what was going on: "Within, all moves; without, nothing moves. It is not advisable to cross the great water." The glory days of our relationship lasted about three weeks, in which we got to talk together and tell each other in broad strokes who we were. We saw each other by chance encounters. He never invited me out, didn't ask for my number. But at that age, I didn't even imagine those were the customs. One afternoon, giddy with the intensity of this previously unknown emotion—like an intoxicating substance circling through every inch of my insides, filling me with a kind of painful bliss—I took a red marker and wrote his name on an index card. Despite the obvious interest he showed in me,

I had convinced myself that he could never like me. When I look at photos from that time, I see a thin, gangly girl with a pretty face. Someone rather attractive, and yet what I saw in the mirror back then was something similar to the caterpillar found dead in my shoe. A slimy and repulsive creature. Sometimes I think that initiating my love life with so little self-love was a bad omen and determined the way in which I would interact with the opposite sex in the years to come. After finding ourselves together almost every day for some time, Oscar stopped showing up as often. It's not that he suddenly stopped seeing me, it's just that he spent less time with me. I soon realized that he had a new friend, Marcela Fuentes, a girl older than we were, a little plump, and much shorter than me, but also much less shy. Every afternoon she'd go to the window of her apartment in the building across the way, right next to Ximena's, and whistle, her hands cupped into the shape of an ocarina. The sound she made was strong enough to cover a fairly wide field. Oscar would respond from his own window, and for a while they would signal to each other like that. I confess I secretly practiced that whistle until I could do it exactly as they did. Sometimes I was even able to sound it from my window, hidden behind the curtains of my bedroom.

My rival was a friend of Ximena's sister, Paula. She belonged to a group of teenagers who got together to sing in a sunny little garden behind their building. Also in that group were my neighbor Florencia Pageiro, whose brother was on the team, and a few boys I didn't know. They were all already in middle school and, to those of us who were not there yet, they seemed like a completely inaccessible group, except for Oscar. I saw them as free people, with much more independence and less confinement than I could then even dream of. The girls wore tight jeans that showed off their feminine figures, or long skirts of super-thin fabric, and scarves from India and leather sandals. According to what Florencia's brother told me one day, what they listened to at home and sang in loud voices in that garden were "protest songs."

One afternoon, while I was coming home caked in mud and sweat from a soccer game, I ran into Marcela in front of Building Six. She came straight out and asked me if I liked Oscar. The possibility that he might be listening or that she might tell him what I said didn't occur to me. It seemed almost like abuse for an older girl and her friend to come at me like that. In the ten-year-old male environment that was my social circle, liking someone was pathetic and a sign of weakness. I didn't have enough experience to tell her it was none of her business and that she shouldn't butt into things that didn't concern her. Instead I told her that Oscar grossed me out. Basically, I kicked the ball with my shin and handed it over to the enemy. The point being that from then on I saw Oscar even less.

More than six months after I joined the building's soccer team, the sports club of our unit started a league. As to be expected, all the boys who played with us every after-noon in the plaza wanted access to real fields and metal goal posts, to a place where players wore jerseys and cham-pionships were held. It all seemed very appealing to me too, but the problem was they didn't let girls play. On top of that, registration was three thousand pesos, and my grandmother was never going to give me that much money just so I could keep disobeying her. My only option, if I convinced them to accept me, was to take the money out of her purse, something I had never done before and that scared me just to think about. But I was prepared to do anything. The day my brother signed up, I made up my mind to go with him to the sports office to argue my case. I said that for months I had done nothing but play soccer and that, despite being a girl, it was the only thing I cared about in the whole world. I asked them to give me a tryout so I could prove that I could play defense as well as any guy. I talked about national soccer and Mexico's performance in the U-20 World Cup, and they still permanently benched me. That afternoon, my brother stayed to train on fields greener and better kept than any I had ever seen in all my ten years. I, on the other hand, went home, dragging my feet along the road. When I thought I had come to a good spot nobody ever went, I sat down on a stone step, buried my face in my hands, and began to cry. I cried timidly at first, then more and more confidently, until I completely let myself go in what seemed like a never-ending flood of tears. A few minutes later, I felt the palm of a hand on my shoulder. A warm and familiar palm that I didn't recognize until I turned around and found myself facing my grandmother.

"Look at you, crying your eyes out!" she said with a surprised expression. "You look like a widow." Her tone was one of reprimand, like always, and yet this time there glimmered a hint of genuine concern. What else could I do but tell her my problem.

Her reaction was totally unexpected, at least by me. Instead of scolding me for still being interested in the wild game for boys, as she had every afternoon since she moved in with us, she listened carefully as I told her about my visit to the club and, once I'd finished, she offered to help.

My grandmother's solution was to write a formal letter of complaint to the director of the sports club.

"You will see how he consents right away," she said, confident in her strategy. Even though her idea seemed totally absurd I didn't dare argue with her. I was ready to do whatever it took to get into the league, and that included taking my grandmother's advice. It was also the first time she had cared about something that involved me and, beyond that, she was ready to be on my side. After criticizing me for so many months, after calling me a tomboy and I don't know how many other names, she finally accepted my affinity for soccer. That, in and of itself, was already a small victory.

As could be expected, the arguments in the letter my grandmother wrote as my guardian to those distinguished people did not invoke equality of the sexes, nor the right of girls to play whatever sport they want. Instead she spoke of how difficult it was for an old woman to take care of two children with an abundance of energy all by herself and of the ordeal she faced. She also wrote that she couldn't watch me during the day and preferred a thousand times over to pay to know her granddaughter was in a safe place dedicating herself to a sport, not in the streets playing with strangers. My grandmother went in person to deliver the letter to the office that had rejected me. On the heading where she had put her address, as typical for every correspondence, I saw she had written "cc: João Havelange, FIFA Director." I had gone with her to the club but preferred to wait outside. I didn't want to face another rejection.

The meeting didn't last more than fifteen minutes. The director accompanied my grandmother to the door with a smile on his lips and asked me which of the different teams I wanted to join. I explained that my brother and the other boys from my building were Vikings and that was the team I wanted to play for.

"Go to the field and ask for Jerónimo, the coach, so he can give you a tryout."

My grandmother didn't take her eyes off me. There was a grim look on her face and it was impossible to decipher her thoughts. When the director left, she gave me a kiss on the cheek. A kiss, Dr. Sazlavski! The first kiss in the entire time she'd been at the house. It was the most unexpected thing in that moment—even more unexpected than my joining the mini-league—and it left my mind blank for a few seconds.

"I'll see you at home," she said as she left. "You'd better pass this tryout now."

It went well. Knowing that it had always been my position, the coach put me on defense. We practiced Tuesday afternoons and had games from ten to twelve on Saturday mornings. I put everything I had into those practices and I don't think my performance was bad at all. Nevertheless, not everyone was pleased with my being there. Anyone who was used to seeing me play in the plaza wasn't surprised, but the team had taken on new players who didn't live in our unit and traveled several miles twice a week to play with us. For them, having a girl on the lineup wasn't only risky, it was also embarrassing. They said we would look ridiculous because of me. Everyone knows it's not so easy to play when your teammates are hostile toward you. Even so, I think I did a good job of holding my own. They kept me on the bench for the first three games and after that would let me in during the second half, as long as we were ahead. Little by little, I was earning my place among the other players. When at last I gained definite legitimacy on the team, a new obstacle arose, foreseeable by many, perhaps, but something I had not at all anticipated: as if it had suddenly taken on a life of its own, my body sabotaged me. The first thing I noticed was a hypersensitivity of my nipples that got worse from rubbing against my jersey. It made chest traps impossible. Every time I took a shot to the chest, I would fall down in pain. I was scared; if that happened in the middle of an official game, the shaming shouts would immediately rain down on me, things like, "Tits, get off the field!" which I had already heard more than once with no provocation beyond my presence.

In a dream one Friday night, I discovered that for the entire time my brother and I had been living with my grandmother, Dad had been living in our country house with a different family. I woke up certain I would find him there and decided to confirm it. What would I have done, Dr. Sazlavski, if, after all that had happened lately, I were to actually see him? Would I have demanded he explain, or reproached him for leaving us to our fate? That morning I got up very early and left the house unseen. I brought with me a change of clothes and a thousand pesos in bills of fifty that I'd taken from my grandmother's cash box. It was the first time in my life that I'd gone through the gates of Villa Olímpia by myself, which ended up being easier than I'd expected. I got a taxi near the entrance and asked the driver to take me to the Taxqueña bus station. Luckily, the taxi driver didn't ask me to tell him the route, like they all usually do, because I didn't have the faintest idea of how to get there. As soon as I stepped inside the station, I walked up to the first window I saw and asked for a ticket to Amatlán, Morelos. Not once did the clerk at the counter ask about my parents. It surprised me that I was walking so freely around the streets and the halls of the station, enormous in my eyes, and no one seemed shocked to see a little girl alone. My entire life, I had heard stories about how children and preteens are kidnapped in our city if they get separated from their families by five inches. As I climbed onto the bus, I had time to realize that I wasn't the only one. Other young kids like me were moving around on their own, unaccompanied. Some were just passengers, others were at work selling gum or carrying luggage. I sat in one of the first seats, and when we arrived I set off wandering toward the center of town for a few minutes, until I recognized a street that would take me straight to the house. I had to walk a half an hour before reaching the wooden outer door. Despite how nervous the idea of finding my father was making me, I also felt exalted by the adventure and proud of myself. I was ready to face whatever. Neither possible outcome, the absence nor presence of my father in this place, would defeat me. It was with this conviction that I rang the bell. I was going to scale the fence if nobody opened the door. The six feet of stones posed no challenge to my feet, so used to climbing trees and scaling all kinds of crevices. I also needed to know what had happened to the house we hadn't been to in these long months. Was somebody still paying the gardener? I had considered almost every possible outcome, except for the one I found when the door finally opened and a woman dressed as a nurse greeted me. It took me a few minutes to be able to speak.

"Did something happen to my father?"

The nurse smiled kindly but didn't answer my question. Instead, she asked what my name was and invited me inside. It felt like a mistake, a time lapse, or something like that. This woman's white uniform, her stockings, and her chunky shoes were all a bad omen. So was her evasiveness.

"Not that I know of," she answered. "He hasn't come here for some time. But you'd better come with me to see his sister, Señora Anita. She talks to him once in a while. Let's go to the office."

My Aunt Anita was my father's older sister. I hadn't seen her in over three years. What was she doing here?

I didn't have a damn clue what was going on, but decided not to demand an explanation and to follow her. The nurse led me to the main room in the house, upstairs, which I had always known as the master bedroom. What I saw on the way increased my bewilderment: everywhere, from the garden to the terrace and around the pool, there were old people. Other nurses were pushing them around in wheelchairs. There was no sign of our dog. They must have tied her up so she wouldn't attack the old folks. I didn't ask, I just continued up the stairs. When I got there, I saw the bedroom was completely transformed into an office: bookshelves, filing cabinets, and tables with documents had replaced the bed and dresser. My aunt was on the other side of the desk. When she saw me, she stood up from her chair and ran over to hug me.

"Love," she said, "what are you doing here?" Her face showed worry and pity. I could have asked her the same question. But I decided to ask something more urgent:

"Where is my dad?"

My aunt hugged me again and told me the same thing as everyone else.

"He's still in the United States. We don't know when he'll be back. But you know who is here? Your grandmother. Do you want to see her?" My heart dropped into my stomach. Was it possible that she had followed me to the bus station? It took me a few seconds to understand that she was talking about my paternal grandmother, the one I hadn't seen in over a year.

"It was your father's idea to turn the house into a nursing home. This way we can take care of your grandmother and earn a bit of money at the same time."

My aunt's explanation seemed to make sense, but seeing it in effect didn't. At least for me, it was maddening to see so many old people in bathrobes and pajamas in the hallways and bedrooms. Throughout the entire building you could smell the shameless odor of urine barely masked by the subtle smell of disinfectant. The current state of our house was proof that everything had been irrevocably turned upside down. On the wall in the living room there was a sign: "Learn to die and you will have learned to live." The phrase would remain stuck in my memory. While we were walking, I took advantage of the silence to ask about Betty, our dog. I was told that she had gone home with the gardener, Guillermo, with the promise that he would return her when asked. I was happy for the dog; the care-taker was a good person and fond of her. She was certainly better off with him and his family than in this home where everyone was waiting around to die.

Anita took me to a patio out back, a spot we had never thought about when the house was ours. That's where my paternal grandmother was, sitting with a vacant expression in a wheelchair. Many months ago, I had heard Dad say that his mother suffered from a mental illness that made her regress to different previous stages in her life, and that there was nothing she nor anyone could do to stop it, but this was the first time that I had seen someone with Alzheimer's.

"Her condition has gotten much worse," my aunt commented, her voice serious. "She can't really talk. But, you know what? I'm sure she's happy to see you."

My grandmother's expression didn't show an ounce of joy. Instead she looked stern, with that downturned mouth her decendents, all of us, have inherited—an accentuated inverted smile. I have it, and so does my brother, my father, and the same Aunt Anita. Years later, my son would show it off from his incubator. My grandmother had become the most defenseless being in the world, unable to decide for herself where and how she wanted to live, like a child, and yet, at the same time, she had an enviable means of escaping to better days. I gave her a little hug like my aunt had given me in the office, and when I did, I recognized the scent of her skin. I remained with her in silence while Anita went off a few feet to explain I don't know what to the nurses. When she came back, I stood behind the wheelchair and kissed the graying hair of my grandmother. It was the last time I was with her.

My aunt asked me if I wanted to spend the night there. She also offered to take me to Cuernavaca, where she lived, to spend the rest of the weekend with her family. But I preferred to return to Mexico City. I didn't want what I had done to come to light back home. My grandmother would get alarmed and, much worse, double her vigilance, restricting this very promising freedom that I had just found. I returned to the apartment that evening like any other Saturday. When my brother asked why I never came to the soccer field that day, I told him that I had not felt like seeing anyone. That was all I said. Once in bed, I went through the images of the day. For the first time in nine months, I was glad to be home.

As could be expected, my self-esteem and family issues also became a problem at school, although, to be honest, I think the situation there had already been bad for a while. For almost three years I had spent my mornings peacefully writing stories, focused on nothing else. When my mother left, writing no longer interested me; nothing but soccer did. All of my vital energy was centered on this sport, allowing me to forget myself and my circumstances.

I don't have many memories of my classmates that year. Some of them had been with me since the beginning, and the relationship I had with them was almost like family. Kenya and Paulina sat at my table. The year before, we had become good friends and still were, except everything was so different. For me, the absence of my parents and the never-ending conflict with my grandmother had transformed me into someone else. Not only did it change the way I dressed and did my hair, it also changed the look on my face. I showed signs of developmental delay. While my classmates knew how to divide and were starting to study fractions, I was still having trouble with multiplication. During the previous school years, there had formed in my mind pools of unfathomable depths like the ones described in fifth-grade geography that I knew nothing about. My personality, prey to the typical changes of puberty, became gloomier, more taciturn. I spoke less. Almost nothing in my life mattered. Nor was I motivated to learn. Instead of writing, I now gave myself entirely to reading. Poe's *Extraordinary Stories* and some of Kafka's short stories were my favorites. I identified fully with the main character in *The Metamorphosis*, since what happened to him was something similar to what had happened to me. One morning, I too woke up with a different life, a different body, not knowing what it was I had turned into. Nowhere in the story does it say exactly what kind of insect Gregor Samsa was, but I quickly gathered it was a

cockroach. He had turned into one; I was one by maternal
decree, if not by birth. As I was reading the book, I began
to research this species at school and discovered its exclu-
sive pedigree, which not many people in my life seemed
to be aware of. Just as Spanish kings descended from the
Bourbons, cockroaches descended from the trilobites, the
oldest inhabitants of the planet. They have survived climate changes, the worst droughts, and nuclear explosions.
Their survival does not imply they haven't known suffering, but that they have learned to overcome it. Reading
The Metamorphosis was confusing. From the first pages, I
couldn't tell if it was a misfortune or blessing what had
happened to the character—who, as if it all wasn't enough,
never displayed any sort of enthusiasm or drama. Like him,
I too inspired some disgust in my classmates. Children are
very perceptive and could clearly distinguish the smell of
unhappiness my body was secreting. Luckily the teacher I
had that year was also perceptive. She realized that something wasn't right and began to give me special attention.
Not only did she understand that I needed help catching
up in school, she also intuited that my anxiety wasn't just
academic but emotional. Very tactfully, she would ask me
questions in order to learn more about my home life. I
told her everything. I told her about the insects that always
appeared to me and about how scared I was of losing my
sanity or what I had left of it. I also told her about *Innocent
Eréndira*. Not once did she reprimand me for having read
a book inappropriate for my age. Rather, she spoke with
praise about the story and its author, then asked me to tell
her more about why I liked the character. That was how I

started talking to her about Ximena and what she had done in front of everyone, and about my admiration for people who find a way to escape their destiny.

"It's better that you want to kill your grandmother than hurt yourself," she advised.

Iris, that was her name, became a source of great support from then on. In the Montessori system, students usually work on their own and teachers only step in to show them how to use unfamiliar didactic material. Thanks to the independence of the other students, Iris could stick with me like a beneficent shadow, never impeding, never moralizing, never disapproving. It was like she set herself on a mission to help me get back on my feet, and I can say that she was successful. In a few months, not only did I catch up to my classmates, but she even taught me the next year's lessons in grammar, geography, history, and math. If there was ever a time I enjoyed this last subject, it was then, when what set me apart from the others and made me different was being able to take the square and cubic roots of incredibly large decimal numbers. When I had surpassed the level of the class, Iris called my grandmother to give her my academic evaluation. My grandmother walked out of that meeting speechless. She didn't want to tell me exactly what had been said, but I figured it was something very good because when we left she granted me the second kiss of her stay.

Shortly after that, my grandmother announced that we would be going with her to visit our aunt and uncle near the US border, in Juárez, a city with a terrible reputation today. Apart from my mother, my grandmother had given birth

to five other children—four more daughters and one son—
who had spread out in different states across the country.
The Juárez ones, as we usually called them, were my Aunt
Victoria's family. A generous and good-natured woman,
Aunt Victoria had always been affectionate and kind to us.
Even though I didn't like the idea of leaving Mexico City
and not having the company of my teacher for a few weeks,
I had very happy memories of visiting that family with my
parents and spending long vacations together. Also, my
aunt was similar to Iris in many aspects: caring and capable
of understanding the minds of children—of putting herself in their place and calming them. Whereas most adults
only saw in me a hostile little girl, insolent and aggressive,
she understood since the beginning that my behavior was
a response to the immense fragility and fear that were suf-
focating me then. She devoted hours of her time to talking
to me. Her words were like delicate and deft fingers stealthily working their way into my head to deactivate a time
bomb. The family had a father who was around, cheerful, and authoritative; a mother devoted to her home and
her family, with a background in psychology and a pen-
chant for humanitarian and charity work; four happy and
good-looking children who played with us; and a house
with a garden in a safe residential development, where you
could skate forever and ride your bike—the Juárez ones
were exactly what we were not. Maybe that's why we were
so drawn to them. To live with them, to stay at their house,
to adopt their ways, to belong for a few days to a functional
family, was like winning a trip to Fantasy Island, the TV
game show in which participants live their wildest dreams,

but only for a few days. And what was more, fifteen minutes away by car was the border and the country that also seemed, in childhood at least, like a marvelous world, with its theme parks, shopping malls, picture-perfect houses, three-level playgrounds, clean movie theaters, and permanent scent of newness. The visit, which was only supposed to last two weeks, went on for more than a month. In this time, my aunt and uncle took us in like two more of their own children and incorporated us into their daily life. Our cousins' school was Montessori, like ours, so in the mornings we joined them there.

The city wasn't as violent as it is now, but there was already talk of kidnappings and drug smuggling. Obviously, we figured it out our own way, from stray phrases we picked up in the middle of adult conversations, and from news on the radio or on the local television channel. One afternoon, some paper money appeared in the backyard, pinned to the clothesline. They were American dollars, not more than thirty dollars in small bills pinned to the metal wire. They waved like flags in the wind. Beyond stretched the desert sky of Juárez. Nobody knew where they came from, or if they were some kind of coded message. My uncle was a surgeon and he saw all kinds of people in his practice. Finally my cousin Jorge, the youngest at about five years old, and whom we had tried to keep out of the whole thing, cleared up the mystery: the dollars were his. He kept hearing talk about money laundering and had decided it was time to wash his savings. So during siesta that day, while the rest of us succumbed to the soporific Juárez heat, he went out to the laundry room and submerged his bills one by one in a bucket of soapy water, then hung them up to dry. We returned home from Juárez stronger and renewed. Being with a loving family with a much more relaxed attitude than my grandmother's had diluted her influence.

My mother came back that summer. We didn't have a lot of time to take in the news. I remember that her presence surprised me, not knowing when I had stopped believing in her return. Both of us had changed in those ten months. She seemed more loose, undone, as if the time spent without her children had noticeably softened her, while time had done the opposite to me. It wasn't just the tense look on my face. My body, too, betrayed several transformations. I had these budding breasts my mother would look at from the corner of her eye, now and again, without saying anything. She didn't like that I curved my back to hide them, but she didn't dare bring it up. Had her long absence taken away her right to criticize me? Maybe, I thought naively, the French had made her more tolerant. Who knows. She didn't breathe a word when my grandmother went off on her long list of complaints about me. It was impossible to know whose side my mother was on. Maybe she refused to align herself with either one of us, something that both my grandmother and I considered an act of disloyalty.

During her first year in France, while living in the university town of Gazelles, Mom had met a guy whom she'd refer to now and then as "my African boyfriend." She talked about him like you would talk about a distant cousin who might very well show up at the house, but there was no way to know for sure. We knew his name was Sunil and, even though he was born and had lived almost his entire life on the island of Mauritius, his family and culture came from India. She also let us know that he was very young, twelve years younger than she was. To put it another way, his age was exactly halfway between hers and mine. Even though Mom never said anything about it, my brother and I didn't rule out the possibility that Sunil would move in with us when we got to France.

My dad also showed up out of nowhere, but just for an afternoon. He brought with him a bag of American toys and, after showing them to us, took us to a park. There he explained why he had spent so much time in the United States: he couldn't stay in Mexico because he was on the run from the police. Nor could he come around the apartment or be with us for very long. They had been tapping the house phone for months. He traveled incognito, under only his first and middle names. He didn't know when the situation would get resolved, or if it would. Despite what you may think, all this information didn't alarm me or make me anxious. It dispelled some of the uncertainty my brother and I had been living with. While many mysteries remained, truth at last came into the home through the windows like a warm and beneficent light, dissolving with its timid glimmer the dampness and filth of doubt.

III.

In October 1984, my mother, brother and I went to live in the south of France. We spent five years in Aix-en-Provence, a city with Roman ruins that saw its apogee in the fifteenth century with the court of King René. Aix is full of remnants of remote splendor. The city is known as one of the most bourgeois and snobby in the country. However, a few miles from its center, there also exist one or two neighborhoods with high crime rates, and it was there we found a house.

Even though I don't remember our good-byes or the flight, the evening we arrived in Aix is still present in my mind. After landing in the Marseille airport, we took a bus that brought us to our new city. That night we slept in a hotel room in the oldest neighborhood downtown. I had just turned eleven and it was the first time I'd been to Europe. Everything around me seemed unusually old, deteriorated, and different. The high windows in our room, the iron heater, the divided bathroom, the chain for flushing the toilet (a real chain with links, and no handle or button next to the water tank to push), the furniture, the pillows (one long one in the shape of a hotdog and other square ones)—everything, in short, was surprising to me. I asked my mother if our school would also be like this, but she didn't know what I was talking about.

"As weird as this," I insisted.

As she had already been to our future school to register us and had toured the facility, she could have given me a better answer. But, while I was trying to find out any new piece of information—anything at all about this unknown country—the poor woman was floundering in an ocean of things that needed to be figured out, some as imminent as dinner that night. Though we already had a school, we were still without a house. Until then, my mother had lived at the university and now needed to apply for housing for married students. It was the middle of October and starting to get cold, or at least it seemed so that evening. Mom left us alone in the room for a few minutes and went to get us something to eat. Dinner was what she found in the only store still open at that hour: plain yogurt in a glass container and a few slices of the thickest and most delicious ham I had ever tasted in my life. I guess there must have been bread as well. I don't remember, but I'll never forget the exquisite taste of the croissant I ate the next morning.

It wasn't easy persuading the secretary at the CROUS housing office to grant us one of the residences reserved for married couples. But my mother was never unpersuasive. Through the half-open door to the office, I listened to her arguing with the woman for fifteen minutes until she had her convinced that two children count at least as much as a husband. So we left with the keys to our new home in hand and an address we were going to right away to drop off all our bags. What the secretary did not explain to us was that the building would smell like insecticide and that the area where we were about to live had the highest crime rate in the city.

Built on the outskirts of Aix, our neighborhood was called Les Hippocampes and was considered the most troubled niche of the urban development zone (the ZAC). It was a new quarter that assembled a unit of buildings around a parking lot in which, every week, its residents set stolen cars on fire in the night. Our apartment was bright, had a nice view, and could even be said to have had a certain charm. Most of our neighbors were of Maghreb origins, but there were also French, Black Africans, Portuguese, Asians, and Roma who'd settled down. As much as we investigated, we were unable to find a single Latino. Rough sights have stayed with me from those days, like the afternoon I ran into a badly beaten young wife. She was on the stairs that went up to the second floor, where you could almost always pick up on a strong smell of cumin emanating from the apartments. Seeing the woman there, hurt, in a place I had always thought of as a refuge, an intimate place par excellence, completely horrified me and I couldn't help but wonder what secrets she must have been keeping for someone to want to reprimand her in this way. It goes without saying that it was henceforth impossible for me to make these stairs the perfect hideout for exploring my body.

Despite what you might think, the development zone our neighborhood belonged to wasn't ugly, not the least bit. It was, in fact, full of gardens and green areas, places for

kids to play, and even an architectural research center created by the father of Op Art, Victor Vasarely, and where an
important part of his work is still housed. While walking
through the neighborhood with my family, people would
often look at us suspiciously because of our excessively
occidental looks; my brother's blond hair and my mother's
light eyes confused them. But when they heard that our
language was different, and particularly when we said we
were from Mexico, they automatically opened up to us the
doors of their sympathy.

The school we enrolled in was not in the same neighborhood, but a little closer to downtown. It was the most
progressive public school in all of Aix and the surrounding
area—a Freinet method institution that boasted prestige
and high standards. It was called La Maréchale, and to
get there from our house all it took was to get on a bus
that stopped in front of our building and to step off at
the entrance to the school. Classes had begun several weeks
before our arrival and that put me at a huge disadvantage:
the pairs of girls that form at the start of school were already
established. The teacher decided to sit me next to a pretty
girl with chestnut hair. Her name was Julie. Her father was
Spanish and they imagined we would understand each
other. A few minutes was enough to see that Julie knew
perhaps ten words of her paternal language—which wasn't
Castilian but Catalan—and that we were not going to be
close, which I attribute not to a difference of nationality,
so much, as to one of self-perception: she was a fairytale

princess, I was Gregor Samsa. By the way, Doctor, the other day I was walking by a school and saw a mother yelling at her son like a drill sergeant. The boy, around three years old, seemed squashed by the shouts of that out-of-control woman. To defend himself, he was sinking his head down and raising his shoulders like someone expecting the roof to fall. I felt a deep sorrow; he made me think of the body and behavior of a cockroach.

Julie's best friend—with whom I would have to compete for the attention of my benchmate—was named Céline Bottier. She wasn't very conventional, you could say. At eleven and a half years old, her long and dark hair was peppered with gray and her face looked like it belonged to an older woman who was graced with a rather serious character. However, unlike me, Céline had a very high opinion of herself and treated Julie with admirable condescension. In homeroom, there were two other foreign girls, a Belgian and a New Zealander. Even though the Belgian was of Flemish origins, the New Zealander and I were the only ones who didn't speak the language.

Weeks before leaving Mexico, my grandmother and mother had warned us to mind our manners in the school cafeteria since French children were extremely well-mannered and traditional. So when we entered the *cantine* for the first time, my brother and I were very nervous, as if facing an assembled jury that might decide to expel us—not only from La Maréchale but from French society. Fortunately, and to our delight, my mother and grandmother were misinformed. As soon as the snack tray with the cold cuts arrived on our first day, the kids swooped in on the meat slices with their dirty hands and, just like that—without cutting the slices up or putting them on a piece of bread—they stuffed them into their mouths, as if their hope was to store as much as possible in their stomachs. Beholding this spectacle, I felt deeply relieved; the French were not the ascetic and smug monsters they'd been made out to be, but regular people, ordinary, even primitive.

I have no doubt that my mother sought in Aix the institution that most resembled our school in Mexico. The percentage of atypical beings was equal, or maybe even higher. But still, as I said before, everything there seemed strange to me. On the one hand, there was the intrinsic Frenchness, and on the other the Freinet system and all its hurdles. The French wrote in a very round cursive using fountain pens with disposable cartridges, which held ink you could erase with transparent markers that had a sickening smell. They used commas instead of decimal points and different figures to represent mathematical operations. It took me months to understand that the functions my classmates were doing underneath the "little house" that looked like the square root symbol were actually just simple double-digit divisions. In Mexico, notebooks are unequivocal: graph paper for math and lined paper for language arts and social sciences. The space between the lines in the latter measures exactly one centimeter and this cannot be changed on a whim. In French notebooks, every page has squares and the space between the lines comes in two different sizes, and for indecisive people like me, knowing where to write presents a dilemma. In the Freinet system, unlike Montessori, there weren't a lot of fun learning materials. It was just some flash cards with questions on different subjects. Another radical difference was that school days in France went until five p.m. Each student worked at his or her own pace, but there were restrictions. Every Monday, we had to set up a "contract" that specified the work we would complete during the week, and it was the teacher's job to check that we fully adhered to our plans. Also on Mondays, we had meetings called "*Quoi de neuf*," in which we could share something we wanted the rest of the class to know. Since I didn't speak French, I was usually left out of these gatherings.

Our school had three yards where we played at recess. There was the main esplanade where each morning we stood in lines before going inside, and two other yards. It wasn't written anywhere, but the students had decided that the biggest and deepest yard, a sloped and unpaved plot, was exclusively for playing marbles; the other square had traces of grass and was reserved for holding soccer matches. In France, they also thought it was a little weird for a girl to play soccer. I'd never played marbles and at first was inclined toward the sport of my childhood, but very soon I stopped playing for the same reasons that had made me give it up in Mexico. And so, gradually, I switched over to marbles, an activity I knew nothing about. The marble scene was run by Dimitri, a boy from the East who had an unmistakable aptitude for managing a casino. He was the one who gave me my first marble and a rough explanation of the rules accompanied by a lot of hand gestures.

This was how I was able to hit the target and win the five other glass spheres that I would play with for the rest of the week. I remember the hurried atmosphere of the place, the jittery back-and-forth of the players, the crack of glass on glass, and the sound of glass rolling over the ground. Even though I have forgotten how much they were all worth, I remember the names of the different marble families: *œil-de-chat, arc-en-ciel, plomb, neige*. These words were also the first I learned in French. To my brother's surprise—and to that of anyone who knows me—I turned out to be not so bad at this marble business (it doesn't feel right to call it anything else), in which sight and precision play such an important role. Maybe Dimitri's gift brought me luck. The point is, in just a few days, I managed to amass a considerable number of marbles of varying shapes and values. To store my new collection, I knit a wool pouch that soon grew dirty on the ground.

Another disconcerting aspect of French schooling caught us off-guard halfway through our first week. It was Wednesday at noon, and instead of heading to the *cant-ine* the kids all rushed out the front door with the same enthusiasm they showed every other day at five o'clock. My brother and I were stuck in this frenzy like people blocked by a protest march. We asked a teacher who spoke a few words of our language if something out of the ordinary was happening, and she tersely answered in textbook Spanish: "On Wednesdays, class finishes at midday. Your mother must know this." According to her, we were getting picked up outside the school, just like everyone else. But Mom never came. The street became less and less populated and we grew used to the idea that we would have to wait for her at the school gate for five hours. One of the last mothers to arrive asked us if everything was all right. When she saw that we didn't speak French, she asked again in Spanish. We told her what had happened and she brought us to her house for lunch.

Her name was Lisa and her son Benjamin was in the same grade as my brother. They lived in a very pretty part of the city, full of single houses that were small but charming. Every piece of their furniture was exotic and flush with the floor, like in illustrations from *The Thousand and One Nights*. She told us that she used to be married to a Moroccan man, her son's father, but things didn't work out between them. Now she was back living in France and much happier. The doorbell rang several times while she was talking and, through the half-open door, we saw another two or three people arrive who seemed to be her friends.

"In this home, Wednesdays are communal. I make couscous like I used to in Casablanca, and whoever wants can come share it with us."

We sat down on some cushions on the floor to eat around a very short table. In the *cantine* I'd seen silverware used as spears, but here cuttlery was nowhere to be seen. The guests put their hands into the giant pot then brought them to their mouths. I was grateful for the invitation that had saved us from spending hours in front of the school. When we finished eating, Lisa served us all mint tea, then she lent me and my brother her phone to let our mother know where we were.

"If she can't come, it's no big deal. You can stay here until whenever."

But Mom came right away, so she too was able to participate in the tea ceremony with the other guests. She immediately took a liking to our host and they exchanged numbers.

As soon as we left, and from that afternoon on, my mother started calling Lisa the *baba cool*, a colloquial term for hippies used in France. There were many hippies in Aix in those days, and there probably still are today, as the city suits them nicely. Lisa brought us unto that universe. She knew many parents at the school and had close relationships to some of them. As we got to know her, we discovered that deep down she was a highly intransigent woman. She couldn't stand anyone with a trace of the bourgeoisie. Her attitude, more than cool, bordered on fundamentalism. Whenever chance brought her to the home of an affluent and conservative family, she would commit acts of class terrorism, like farting loudly at a New Year's Eve dinner, or dropping her pants to pee in the pool. But with us, she was a perfect lady. We kept visiting her the whole time we lived in Aix, and even after. Sometimes she invited me to go out as if I were a friend, and we'd drink coffee before going to see an art film. Through her I discovered Pedro Almodóvar, whose *What Have I Done to Deserve This?* I still remember perfectly, despite never having seen it again.

Even though my mother's boyfriend didn't live with us, he slept over a lot. As soon as I met him, I knew that we had nothing in common, not even a mutual interest in faking a diplomatic relationship. If Sunil's strategy with my brother was talking soccer and race cars, with me it was pretending I wasn't there. Maybe the small age gap between us bothered him, maybe he was scared that an emotional bond between us might look suspicious to my mother, or maybe he found my presence insipid or insignificant. Who knows. His influence on my life was mainly musical and culinary. When he stayed over, the air was full of strong smells like fenugreek and turmeric. He'd often blast Pink Floyd, Bob Marley, and a band called Barcklay James Harvest that I've never heard anywhere else. He would often cook homemade curry with coconut milk. It was Sunil's recipes my mother taught me every time when, in the divvying up of domestic chores, it was my turn to cook. You could call Sunil a communist. He had long and very black hair, a prominent nose and almond-shaped eyes. He was tall, skinny, and dark-skinned. He played soccer at the university, and at home he would lose himself in baffling rituals like staring at the sun and making hand gestures while breathing through only one nostril.

"He's doing yoga," my mother explained whenever we'd watch him, intrigued and seeking an explanation for his unexpected behaviors.

Sunil's family, one of the wealthiest on the island he was from, did not at all approve of his relationship with my mother, whose main defect was not that she was divorced or older, but that she had been raised in a casteless society. But she still went with him to Mauritius several times.

Between the bus stop and school there was a store that sold candy and stationary (in Mexico, candy stores are usually also cigarette shops or pharmacies). I'm convinced the store merchandise one associates with childhood sweets is directly related to adult interests. I, for instance, like the pens and notebooks with heavyweight paper that I know almost as well as I know over-the-counter drugs and deodorants. I should mention that for the first year, French candies tasted a little bland to me. None of them were spicy, florescent, or radioactive-looking, and this greatly diminished my appetite for them. Their names accentuated their differ-ence from those of my country. Instead of Pulparindo and Burbuzest, there they had fruit or animal names: *oursons*, *minibananes*, *fraises tagada*, as if you couldn't easily distin-guish them by the generic substance of which they were made. In short, they lacked mystery and, above all, the scat-ological aspect that brought repulsed looks to grownups' faces and increased their appeal. With time I developed a taste for these mild-mannered unambiguous sweets. One of my favorites was the Malabar, a piece of gum that came with a tattoo you could put on yourself with spit, just by licking it and sticking it on your arm. Another was a long caramel called Carambar that tasted like our *chiclosos de leche* but of better quality.

Our Mexican roots seemed to stir up a curiosity in the kids at school. Whenever they could, they would ask us if we still wore feather headdresses, if we lived in pyramids, or if people were used to driving cars. To impress them, I told them whatever came into my head. I told them there weren't many cars and that to get to school we often traveled by elephant.

Time passed and the Belgian girl went back to Belgium. This left a vacancy in the friendship with the New Zealander that I didn't let go to waste. Her name was Nathalie O'Callaghan. We had a few things in common. In addition to being foreigners, she was as tall and ungainly as I was, and her brother Michael, who was the same age as my brother, was also a young soccer star. They lived in a neighborhood very similar to ours. Their parents were also separated, but at least they knew their father's whereabouts. Unlike everyone else, Nathalie and her mother were not scared to come to our house or to walk about in the area, among the possible criminals. I remember, one afternoon as we were walking toward my house, we came across a tough girl. Everything about her—her black denim clothes, studded bracelets, work boots, and irritable expression—seemed designed to inspire fear. When we saw her, we couldn't think of anything better to do than to mess with her. It was pretty fun until her sister showed up. For the first time in my life, I was hit by people my own age and the experience very much differed from the hard whacks my mother occasionally dealt me. Rachida and Besma, the girls from the ZAC, gave us a well-deserved beating and, instead of being humiliated by it, I felt like there was something epic and exalting about the incident. Not shedding a tear, Nathalie and I walked to my house with red faces and accelerated heart rates. Luckily no one was home. So there we sat, nostalgically drinking chocolate milk and talking about the customs that come from living in a country colonized by white people, where there were things like KFC, McDonald's, and Disneyland—things that brought us together and that made us incomprehensible to French kids.

I finished elementary school at La Maréchale and the following year my mother enrolled me at the local middle school, known by the name Collège du Jas de Bouffan. *Jas* is a Provençal term that refers to a sheep pen, or sheepfold. Decades ago, the place had been a summer residence that Paul Cézanne's father had bought and which the painter had later inherited. At this school, teachers were no longer progressive and liberal, but the opposite. They tried at all costs to impose an iron discipline to mitigate the rebellious and violent atmosphere that reined among the students. I was twelve at the time. I hadn't yet gotten used to the metamorphosis my body was undergoing. My clothing was outdated and my haircut looked more like Spike Lee's than Madonna's (the model of beauty for the girls in my class). I wore huge pink thick-rimmed glasses, spoke French with a Latino accent, and had an unpronounceable name that sounded vaguely like a French island lost in the Caribbean. The corrective patch yielded results, above all in diminishing my strabismus. Because of the patch, my eyes lined up for almost ten years, but when I stopped using it my eye became accustomed to the delights of lethargy and increasingly turned toward my nose with an exasperating indolence. Forcing it to move would have involved covering up the good eye and thus subjecting myself to the very thing I had so despised and suffered as a young child. So I had to choose between disciplined torture for the sake of physical normalcy—which was never going to be absolute—and resignation. On the other hand, my left eye strove to take in as many sights as possible, all on its own. This frenetic activity produced a trembling movement medically known as nystagmus and which people tended to interpret as insecurity or nervousness. Not even the nerds would come near me. Again I was an outsider, if I'd ever stopped being one.

At this new school, there were kids from many different countries, mostly African. I remember Kathy, a dark-skinned girl with a stunning smile and robust breasts who came from the island of Reunión. There were many Moroccans, a few Asians, and also some Indians. The best student in my class, whose name I have forgotten, was from Rajasthan. She scored the highest grades, even a few 20/20s, which are nearly impossible to get in the French system. One day, in which she had been awarded one of these marks of genius on a particularly difficult physics exam, I asked her if she knew what she wanted to do when she grew up. She answered without thinking twice:

"I've already figured that out. I'm going to be an assistant pedicurist, like my aunt."

She was an ingenuous girl, discreet and quiet, who spent her free time studying, but I still had a hard time believing that she wasn't pulling my leg with that response. Later, she

explained to me that her aunt was the only woman in the
family who worked and that, unlike every other occupation, dedicating oneself to the beauty of other women was
not looked down upon in her clan. A few months later,
there was a school program for us to get some work experience in the profession of our choice, and this girl—whom
for her academic record alone NASA or Aerospace would
have taken had she applied—opted to work in a salon just
as she had said she would. There was more to these real-life
work experiences than a desire to learn. Many of the kids
who studied at my school were advised to quit at the end
of the term in order to apprentice at a trade. I guess the
teachers were terrified of the possibility they'd never finish
their education and instead jump with both feet into the
criminal activities some of them were already dipping their
toes into. There was a lot of frustration in the atmosphere
at that school, and it would escalate into verbal and physical violence as soon as backs were turned. The cafeteria
was the favored place for those attacks. They sat us down at
random—giving no consideration to similarities of personality, race, or age among us—around a long table that no
one seemed to be keeping an eye on and that almost always
ended up under the rule of some Mafioso-type boy. For the
entire year, my table was under the rule of a young Italian
with sky-blue eyes, Cello, whose last name was pronounced
"Sheh-lo," and who amused himself by tormenting the
youngest and least clever among us. He was always claim-
ing my dessert or the pieces of cheese that were meant for
me. He fired breadcrumb pellets into our glasses of water.
But the most insufferable joke this hooligan-in-training

played on me didn't take place in the cafeteria; it happened outside at recess, and its consequences were far more devastating. I'll talk about that in a little while. To survive in this climate, I had to adapt my vocabulary to the argot—a mix of Arabic and Southern French—that was spoken around me, and my mannerisms to those of the lords of the *cantine*. When you're twelve, time still moves slowly. Even though I came from a well-off and educated family, after I lived with poor immigrants for a few years, then became a poor immigrant myself, I ultimately identified with this new condition and its environment.

Every year, the mobile homes of the Roma would settle for a few months behind my new school. One afternoon, my brother had to walk home because of a transportation strike and he ran into a couple of Roma boys. Based on the description he gave when he got home, they must have been about twelve, while he had just turned nine. He told us that, seeing him, one went in front and the other behind to intimidate him. Then they told him to take off the watch and the jacket he was wearing and to hand them over. My brother called on the solidarity between foreigners; he told them he wasn't French and that he had come from Mexico with his mother and sister in search of a better life, just like them.

"And your father?" one of the boys asked.

"He had to stay in Mexico," my brother responded. "We didn't have enough money for him to come too."

The most incredible part of the story wasn't that they

believed him, but that they gave him back his things, amicably and with a handshake. There are rules among the marginalized.

At school there was also a group of French students who stood out among all the other "ethnic fauna," as the headmaster often called us. This group was made up of some twenty students who lived in the rural areas surrounding Aix, most of them in residential neighborhoods, and who clearly belonged to another economic class. These kids—from Ventabren, Éguilles, and similar towns—rode to school in fancy buses, wore brand name clothing, and, most importantly, kept to themselves.

Even though we'd been in France for over a year, Mexico remained omnipresent in our lives. Unlike other immigrant families, we kept speaking Spanish at home, unless my mother's boyfriend was there, and sometimes even then. It's not that we were always thinking about the life we had left behind, or that we were comparing Mexico City to Aix—we almost never did. Rather, from time to time, our country would have a huge breakthrough role as a main character on the international scene. One day, when we came home from school, we found our mother glued to the TV with a stunned expression I'd rarely seen on her face. The news bulletin showed images of the Mexican capital turned into a pile of rubble. Entire buildings had collapsed. According to the reporter, several factories, some luxury hotels, and one of the most important hospitals in the country had been destroyed. The public ambulances and Red Cross were not enough to help the great amount of people buried alive beneath the devastation. I thought of my father first, then of my grandmother, and for the first time in a year and a half I didn't feel an ounce of resentment. I thought of my aunts and uncles, and of the friends at school I had left behind. I also thought of Iris, my beloved teacher, and I imagined her trying to flee the school building followed by a string of kids. We tried many times to call our family to find out if they were still alive but it was useless, the phones weren't working. There was no way to speak to anybody there; the entire city was cut off. I realized my mother was making an immeasurable effort to remain calm and all it did was scare me more. I couldn't keep myself from imagining everyone I knew sepulchered beneath the remains of our capital. The past may have been utterly extinguished by little more than two minutes of terrestrial oscillation. And at the same time, there was something unreal in all of it: in our living room the sun came in through the high windows like it did every fall afternoon; the fountain remained on, filling the place with its bucolic sound; and outside you could hear the laughter of happy, carefree children. My brother chose to forget all about it and went to play in the hallway with his foam ball. Meanwhile, my mother spun the telephone dial again and again. The consulate provided an information line, and even though it was impossible to discover each relative's fate, the line was able to roughly tell us which streets had been affected and which had not. Of course, the line was always busy. When at last she got through, the question my mother asked totally baffled me:

"Can you tell me, miss," she said with anguished urgency, "if there were any deaths at North Prison?"

After that, she asked about the streets her family lived on.

When she put down the receiver, she seemed lighter by several tons.

"You don't have to worry," she said, "your father is alive."

Even though I'd never heard of North Prison, I didn't need to think about it long to know it had to be a jail. Twenty-eight months of silence and ignorance were illuminated by a single phrase. That's how the earthquake also took down my last remnants of naivety and innocence. I spent the next few days digesting the news that neither devastated nor infuriated me, as one might expect, but which did drastically upset the worldview I had created for myself until then. My mind took its time to erase my father from the San Diego map and to put him back on the ground in the capital of Mexico, where he had been judged and ultimately detained. During these days of adjustment I spoke very little. When I did, it was to ask Mom about some detail I was trying to understand. It didn't really matter to me what Dad had done or what he used to do so much as how his health was or how he was feeling. Above all I wanted to know the day he would be released, which we all assumed to be imminent.

A few weeks later, for the first time in two years, I received a long letter from my father. I would have loved to have kept it, to be able to reproduce a few of its lines. It was obvious that this letter, which didn't explain anything or dispel our possible concerns, was written in a moment of great despair and catharsis. He told us that it was cold and the dampness in his cell was unbearable. He also told us that he hadn't been able to move his foot for over a week, one of his toes had turned purple then black from a blood clot, and he had gone to the doctor who had given him some medicine but he had yet to feel its effect. He also told us that we, his children, were the best things in his life. Every morning he remembered us all together and those loving memories helped keep him alive, without losing hope. By the time the card arrived, a month and a half after the postmarked date, he had probably gotten better, either from the medicine or from a surgical amputation of the black toe, and still the card was like a cry for help suspended in time and reached our ears as such. Had I been older and had my own money, there is no doubt I would have hopped on the first flight to Mexico to go see him, but at that age and in my circumstances the only thing I could do was respond to the letter and wait another month and a half for it to reach him. Thus I began a drawn-out correspondence with my father, beneficial to us both, and the physical evidence of which is lost now somewhere in the ocean, but not forgotten.

The second time Mexico burst onto center stage was less dismal, true, but also very intense. It happened the following year during the 1986 World Cup, which my brother and Sunil followed unblinkingly on the same television where months earlier we had seen images of our destroyed city. Even though we were living far away, everything seemed to revolve around this country that had been laid to waste. I perfectly remember Pique, the World Cup mascot, because my brother and I shared the nickname during the last few months of our classes, and also Mar Castro, the "Chiquitibum," whom all the boys brought up in the cafeteria, asking me if I knew her personally. I also remember the final and the controversial goal by Maradona, whom we were rooting for at home because Mexico had lost and Sunil couldn't stand the German team. Contrary to what could be expected from me, I didn't follow the World Cup with the passionate abandon that one year before I undoubtedly would have shown. So much had happened recently that there wasn't any room left in my spirit for strong emotions.

IV.

We spent our first vacation in Mexico at my grandmother's big ramshackle house. Several changes had taken place. Beyond the rubble left by the earthquake, visible everywhere, there had been collapses on the familial scale too. We found one of these small yet eloquent changes on arriving from the airport. On the way, our grandmother kept telling us that a surprise awaited us on the roof of her house. As soon as she parked the car my brother and I climbed to the third floor to see what it was. There we found Betty, who two years ago had disappeared on the streets of Amatlán. When she saw us, she started barking with joy and lovingly jumping on us. Our grandmother said it was the first time in months she had looked so happy. And later, in a tone mysterious and amused, she said to me, "They say dogs look like their masters and she turned out identical to you."

We stayed there almost the entire summer vacation, from the end of June until late August. My mother returned to France almost immediately to start writing her thesis. Despite how difficult living together had been a few years

earlier, staying at our grandmother's house wasn't as awful
for me as one might think. This time, we were both relaxed,
knowing it was only for a relatively short time. And in a
few weeks my cousins would come to visit for fifteen days
and the house would be happy, full of kids of all ages. Like
always when our relatives came, my grandmother moved
her belongings from room to room to accommodate them.
Purses and shoes from the forties circulated once again
through the hallways and foyer in a trajectory impossible
to interpret much less predict. However, this time the wave
contained a new and troubling element: among the newspaper clippings, and the hats and clothing that poked out
of all those boxes, I recognized my own toys. Apparently,
everything we had decided not to bring to France with us
had been sucked into the maelstrom. My childhood now
formed a part of that shifting past, and yet was still present
in the house like a sand pit ready to swallow everything if
you take your eyes off it. But the most memorable event that
took place during the trip was our longed-for reunion with
my father. Now that his whereabouts had been revealed, we
could visit him at last.

Dad was locked up in a preventative detention facility
known as Reclusorio Preventivo Norte, or RENO, a prison
for those who were not yet formally charged. While awaiting his sentencing, he had the privilege of wearing beige,
a vague and indistinct color halfway between excretory
brown and innocent white. In the prison for the con-
demned, we later learned, inmates wore navy blue, a color
that didn't allow for ambiguity. My grandmother, who had
already been to see him, was our Virgil into that institution,

a place not exactly a hell, but more a purgatory and also a kind of casino where luck could favor you in a flash or leave you in the worst kind of ruin. Many influential prisoners, the Mafia and drug traffickers, lived there in that decade, in cells befitting their eccentric and luxurious standards of living. My grandmother decided to take us there, but not by the sterile car nor taxi cabs she often rode. She chose, and I think she was right, to carry us by the route most visitors took to get there—public transportation—which back then was old, dirty, and unreliable. So we embarked on an arduous procession across the entire city on the roads that for Luis Buñuel evoked France's *cour des miracles*, districts where people lived in flimsy constructions of tin laminate or cardboard and warmed their hands over hotplates. Near the prison, you could see a display of foods, watches, bags, stuffed animals, underwear, videocassettes, and decorations for the home, similar to the kind often found around some metro stations. Our ride turned out to be effectively transitional and also desensitizing. Because of it, when we reached the prison gates we weren't terrified, and we weren't unnerved.

The prison was gray and fairly rectangular or square in shape, a comb-like structure as it's often called in architecture. There had originally been ten dormitories laid out side by side, in addition to the admissions dormitory and another for observation and classification, through which every new inmate inevitably had to pass before being assigned a permanent dormitory. To get inside, we had to stand in different lines and wait our turn. At the start of each of these waits, we were asked to write our names on a list and to write the name of our imprisoned family member under a column marked "Offender," in a strange ritual of initiation or affiliation. They also asked the nature of the relationship, and so we wrote, five or so times, the word "father" on lists with names of our capital's alleged criminals. In that moment, it felt to me as if there had been a monumental mistake, an arbitrary injustice dealt by the hand of fate that we had to face as I had the divorce, Ximena's death, and my mother's going to France. I don't know what your thoughts are, Dr. Sazlavski, but, for me, the supposed wonder of childhood that people talk about is one of those dirty tricks that memory plays on us. As different as one life is from another, I am sure that no childhood is entirely pleasant. Children live in a world of circumstances decided for them. Others decide—the people they are with, the place they live, the school they attend, and even the food they eat every day. My father being a prisoner was just more of the same. No use crying or arguing.

Those in line outside and in the waiting room were, almost all of them, of the female sex. They were mothers, sisters, wives, and even mothers-in-law—or, as in my grandmother's case, ex-mothers-in-law—who came to visit the inmates. Many brought thermoses with still-warm stews, tortillas, and supplies for the week, and that's why it took so long for things to move; each item had to be inspected to see if it contained weapons or drugs. It wouldn't be the first time. My father told us that one woman often hid marijuana in her son's diapers, so that her husband could live off the sales. As far as I remember, we brought neither food nor pot. But what we did do was wear more formal clothing than usual. My brother, who was nine years old at the time, had on a navy blue sports jacket and I wore a skirt and white tights—a ridiculous or at least inappropriate getup that did nothing but emphasize how we didn't belong. We weren't the only *güeros* there. Other middle- and upper-class people were also waiting in the room and stood out like white mice in a crate of squirrels. Not that there was any complicity between us; everyone acted like they had no idea how they got there. Not even within each social class in Mexico does there exist a sense of belonging or fellowship. "Solidarity" was a word virtually unknown in those days, and would soon be completely discredited by a president. Even though we didn't have a grocery basket or bag, we still had to go through several searches of our clothing and of my grandmother's purse. They made us take off our shoes and inspected our socks. Rough jailkeeper's hands passed over my entire body to make sure I wasn't smuggling anything in. After this preamble, we were at last allowed into the space of the prisoners to be reunited with my father in a huge dining hall. Those who lived in the prison often called it "Reno Aventura" in allusion to the amusement park, Reino Aventura, built a few years earlier near where the Rinaldi sisters lived.

Astonishing are the tricks of memory. I know, for example, that I must have felt sorry for my father, seeing him at one of the tables with his eyes brimming with tears and the emotion of being with us, and yet my memory would have me believe that the austere and clean place wasn't so bad, and that being locked up in there wasn't so unbearable, as if truncating the distant images could mitigate a pain from the past. What hurts to remember are not the circumstances, which thankfully are different today, but rather the acknowledgment of what we felt before, and that, nobody, not even amnesia, not even the strongest painkiller, can change. The pain remains in our conscience like an air bubble with contents intact, awaiting invocation or, in the best-case scenario, to be allowed to come out.

After a few minutes of happy and emotional reunion (apparently we had grown and changed a lot since the last time we met), my father started joking around about his situation. He told us the nicknames of some of the prisoners and the most shocking and strange anecdotes they had told him. He smelled different but looked healthy and well-fed, something my grandmother reiterated several times. He still had the incredible sense of humor that had always marked him and often emerged during the greatest moments of sadness in our family history—at wakes, preoperative periods, and such—to meet the agony of our loved ones. Maybe it would take a while for someone who doesn't know him to understand: it's not at all a flippant attitude, but an astonishing ability to distance himself from the moment at hand and to laugh at it. While he did talk about how the guards were corrupt and how hard it was to find good company, he saved the worst stories for another time. Only years later would he tell us about the incidents of mistreatment and extortion he had witnessed.

My brother, who hadn't said a word the entire time, at last let out the question that seemed to be tormenting him:

"Dad," he asked, "where are the murderers?"

My father explained that in Dorm Five there were drug

traffickers, and in Dorm Three, murderers. It was tacitly accepted that not every manslaughter could be judged the same way—some were involuntary or negligent, others committed in self-defense and therefore necessary, and still others were crimes of passion. That said, all the inmates did condemn and scorn rapists. Whenever a man accused of rape came to the prison, he had to pass through a long makeshift gauntlet of prisoners hell-bent on hitting him in the head and face. Dad told us they had placed him in Dorm Four, "the most laid-back one," reserved for white-collar criminals.

Around that time, they had caught two of Mexico's biggest drug lords of the eighties, known as Ernesto "Don Neto" Fonesca and Rafael Caro Quintero, along with a whole host of collaborators, so Dorm Nine was left entirely in their charge, and the rest had to be relocated to annexed buildings. A few times a week, there were parties organized for the drug lords with a brass band that played until dawn.

My memory of the visit—once we were actually together—is rather happy and tender. It was the reunion I had so badly needed. The food in prison wasn't as terrible as you might think. A trio played in one of the farthest corners of the patio, giving the place ambience with their romantic songs, but not to the point of annoyance. At around six p.m. they announced it was time to leave. We said good-bye, wishing out loud that our next visit would be somewhere else. Once again, we had to get into long lines with people all squished together. Our grandmother decided we'd return in a taxi and so the trip home was much shorter.

What had my father done? What crime was he accused

of, exactly? This is something that I—far from being indif-
ferent about—didn't want to know. I could have asked my
mother or grandmother, who would have answered me
without hesitation, but I didn't want to. They would have
definitely given me their own versions of the facts and their
own moral judgments (my grandmother's that of 1900, my
mother's that of the seventies). I had the chance during our
visit to the prison to ask my father for his own point of view
and to hear his story from his own lips—and still, I chose
not to know. I wanted to show the world that, like his for
me, my love for him was unconditional and I couldn't care
less about whatever fault they accused him of, or whether
he was guilty or innocent. This was an unspoken agreement I made with myself, and I got the feeling my brother
adopted a similar attitude. I knew perfectly well who my
father was. I knew he was a loving and responsible person
who had always attended to and cared for his family, even
his ex-wife. I knew he was a generous man with a heart of
gold, who moved by a child or old woman in need would
empty his pockets; who didn't cheat at games, not even for
fun; and who almost always kept his word. Nevertheless, I
wonder, Dr. Sazlavski, if deep down in this stance of mine
hid a great fear of discovering something I wouldn't like,
something terrible and vile. Later I learned the crime levied
against him was embezzlement, a word I had never heard
before and that still sounds to me more like a venereal dis-
ease than a social defect, and all it means is the diversion
of funds. In the years following my father's release, I got
the chance to talk to him about his time in prison. He
swears—and I believe him unquestioningly—that if he had

ever had the money he was accused of taking, he could have easily bought his freedom in our corrupt society. The truth is my father was left without a cent or a place to lay his head. Part of his sentence was to give up all of his belongings and properties. Luckily, we were able to hold onto an apartment and our country house, which after the divorce had been put in my mother's name and today represents a significant part of our family inheritance.

Our dog Betty was not happy in Mexico City. Her story reminded me of Heidi's, the little girl from the Swiss Alps, who after having grown up in the country free to chase badgers and to run around as she pleased was forced to live cooped up in the city of Frankfurt. Despite how happy Betty was to see us again, she was thin and her doggy face wore an expression of resentment. Even though we visited her every morning, it wasn't enough to keep her spirits up. Normally we would have taken her out for a walk twice a day like any other dog, but we weren't allowed out by ourselves. My grandmother argued that bringing a German sheperd down the metal stairs from the roof to the house, then down the back stairs to get to the street, was not only a hassle but torture for the dog. It's true that Betty's body was too big, but she was also gutsy. At night we'd often hear her howling in sadness and boredom from the cement surface, where the only things to look at were a neighbor's garden and the constant flow on the arterial road below. We were told to tether her because she had already tried to escape by jumping from roof to roof for an entire block until she found a service staircase. Betty's attitude made great sense to me and was, at least according to my grandmother, where our resemblance was greatest.

Shortly after hearing this story, and after my first visit to jail, I climbed to the roof and untied Betty. She didn't waste her opportunity. She immediately ran away and was missing for over a week. Seven days of remorse passed in which I confessed my responsibility to no one. Finally, one morning we found her sitting in front of the house. She was waiting for us to let her in. The vet came to make sure she hadn't caught mange or anything of the like during her jailbreak, but the only thing our dog had gotten was irrefutably pregnant.

After that summer we returned to Aix. The heat in France was still at its peak, making it impossible to sleep under a sheet at night. I was back in the same school and entering the *5ème*, which in Mexico would have been the second year of middle school, or seventh grade. That year, in filling out the registration form, my mother told us that our father's professional occupation corresponded to the word "psychoanalyst." "Prisoner" wasn't a job, to begin with, and besides, it would have aroused all kinds of unfounded suspicions. What would we do if we were assigned to a social worker, "one of those witches," as my mother called them, for a psychological evaluation? One had to think of everything. Although she never openly admitted it, I think Mom was scared, and rightfully so, that we wouldn't pass such an exam.

In the *5ème*, I was still a withdrawn girl, borderline anti-social, but in my homeroom there appeared an individual similar to me in temperament and interests, and with whom, oddly enough, I immediately hit it off. His name was Blaise. He was blond and pretty short. Until this year—and since time immemorial—the boys had been shorter than the girls. But now, beginning with the grade above us, most of them were showing noticeable changes: upper lips started to cover in a dark fuzz; voices, once tinged with strange and incontrollable modulations, stabilized; and limbs, along with backs, in many cases took on more bulk. That's why many of the girls my age arranged themselves at recess at strategic points in the yard from which they could watch the rugby or handball games whenever the competitors were the boys from the *3ème* and *4ème* (grades in France go down, not up). Those who made the biggest fuss over testosterone were the Reunionese Kathy and her friend Mireille, originally of Pontoise, whose skin, milky and covered in acne, made her look like one of those cheeses that have been aged too long and grown bulgy. Her blue eyes were the only truly human element in the shifting surface of her face. Both girls fervently admired the male gender of almost every generation, including the professors and other students' fathers. Into their textbooks they would often slip gossip magazines targeted at girls our age that published advice on how to use makeup and weild accessories. I had a good relationship with them but not a close one. Sometimes, when class was particularly boring, or when I looked nervous about an exercise on the blackboard in algebra class, they would see to it that one of these magazines was passed from hand to hand

to land on my desk. I remember in particular one nota-
ble article that discussed the right way to practice kissing
with tongue, which in French we called "rolling a shovel."
The author advised practicing solo for a while with half a
squeezed orange in order to develop the necessary dexter-
ity and sensitivity in the lips. However, for the real thing,
you couldn't forget to stick your tongue out far enough to
meet his tongue, but not so far that it would be uncomfortable for him. At that moment you would begin the
spinning that in a French kiss seemed to be at the heart of
the matter. It was important to find synchrony in spinning
with his tongue, to strike the same speed, and to hit reverse.
I remember that when I finished the article I lifted my head
and looked at the entire class pretending to be absorbed in
the equation. I looked at my classmates, trying to figure out
how many of them, and especially *who*, had already been
through this critical and defining ritual. It needs to be said
that, had I done a survey, most of them would have lied; at
that age, it was mortifying to confess a lack of experience.
The words *pucelle* and *puceau*, which both referred to someone who was still a virgin, were the worst insults you could
receive at my school. You could be a top *pucelle* or bottom
pucelle: "top" meant you'd never kissed and "bottom" meant
you'd never slept with anyone. Most of the girls, with the
exception of the boldest, preferred to assign themselves to
the latter category, almost none to the former, and never to
both unless your family was extremely religious. Despite her
deformed face, I was sure that Mireille had already kissed
several boys. You saw it in the confidence she had talking to
older boys, the very confidence the rest of us lacked; it was

like she knew them inside and out. Kathy, for her part, was one of the sexiest girls in the whole school and there were rumors that for a few months she'd been dating a boy in the *4ème*, but from a different school. There was also Ahmed, a boy from Algiers who had been held back two years and ended up in our class, and who pursued my classmates like a rooster in a henhouse. Except for these three experts, it was hard to guess if anyone else had any significant experience with the opposite sex. To me, the idea alone was equal parts enticing and repulsive. I was dying to be in the arms of one of those *4ème* guys and to kiss like I was eating an orange in the sun, but the whole business with the tongue and spit, and the fragility and the exposure in the moment bordered on unbearable.

Blaise was not one of the boys who were all muscle, not at all. I didn't like him in the least and it was clear that he felt something similar toward me. I guess that's what made us close. Some swear that genuine friendship between men and women doesn't exist. I'd like to know your opinion, Doctor, because it's a notion I completely disagree with. Throughout my life I've succeeded in establishing a strong complicity with some men, almost as strong as what I now have with my best female friends. Blaise's presence that year meant a way out of solipsism. By October, we were sitting together for almost every subject. We also sought each other out in the free time between lunch and class. Recess, however, I spent alone, walking from one end of the playground to the other, greeting the kids I knew but never feeling good enough with any group to stick with them for more than five

minutes. I remember that on one of these restless mornings, Cello, the older boy with whom I shared my lunch
table, came up to me out of nowhere oozing friendliness.
After making small talk for a few minutes, he told me
he had a confession: Sebastien, his best friend, wanted
to meet me and had asked Cello to make it happen. The
recess bell cut short what he was saying.

"Anyway, come over one of these days and I'll introduce
you," he suggested before leaving.

My bewilderment was such that when the lines started
forming in front of the door, I remained in the same spot
in the middle of the playground. I had to struggle to piece
together the fragments of my awareness to make it back to
homeroom. I had seen Cello's friend many times and could
easily place him. He was, in my opinion, one of the most
attractive boys in school, which made the supposed confession seem unlikely. Why would this boy, who had his choice
among the different African and blond queens of the school,
have his eye on one of the untouchables who surreptitiously
prowled the playground? I couldn't believe it, so I decided
to seek counsel. Mireille and Kathy looked at each other in
astonishment. They too easily placed the candidate.

"It doesn't makes sense," I said, trying to be realistic.

"But neither does love," responded Mireille, in a decid-
edly optimistic tone. "Even if you don't know it," her
cheese-mouth added, "you're a very pretty girl."

"Maybe he's interested in Mexico," remarked the less
enthusiastic Reunionese girl.

It had never occurred to me that being Mexican could
make me interesting to a boy in the *4ème*.

Then I remembered the dialogue with Marcela in Villa Olímpica, in front of Oscar's building, a few years before. I didn't want the same thing to happen again and to make Sebastien feel rejected without giving him a chance.

"Why don't you write him a letter?" Kathy suggested. Her friend agreed.

"A letter! Why?" I asked, taken aback.

"To tell him that you like him too, but that you've never gone out with a guy and don't have a lot of experience."

I had never mentioned my experiences with boys to those two. I told myself that if it was so obvious to them that I was a stupid *pucelle*, it would be to him too. Why add insult to injury?

"That way you break the ice," assured Kathy. "If you want we can help you, but not with spelling."

That same afternoon, at lunchtime, instead of meeting up with Blaise in the study hall, I sat down on a bench to draft the famous letter. The girls reviewed it later and changed a few irrelevant phrases. I finished cleaning it up after dinner, while pretending to focus on my homework. I decorated the page with butterfly stickers that I had in my desk drawer to symbolize what I was feeling inside. That night, when the lights were turned off in our living room, I told my brother what had happened. We weren't very close in those days, but we always had the unspoken rule that for things serious and imponderable we could count on each other. He patiently listened to the details of my account and to a summary of the letter.

"You don't have a chance," he said emphatically. "Sebastien has never taken you seriously."

"How do you know?" I asked, trying to hide how offended I was.

"He's in the *4ème*, he's the best rugby player in the school, all the girls are after him. You're in the *5ème*, you're a *pucelle*, and besides, you're pretty ugly."

"You're a *minot* in the *6ème* with a pea-brain," I retorted, "who doesn't know anything about love and how illogical it is."

I couldn't sleep that night. With a light beneath the quilt, I spent almost eight hours reading *The Ice People* by René Barjaval, a novel Blaise had recommended to me. Even though it was science fiction and took place at the North Pole in a future era with great advances in space technology, the story could not have been more romantic. It only heightened my level of expectation about the encounter I believed to be in the making.

I gave Cello the letter the next day, in the cafeteria, and he looked at me with a complicit smile.

"How about you come over and I'll introduce you right now?" he suggested. I didn't have the nerve for that; the letter had used up all the bravery at my disposal.

Three days went by before I had any word from the boys. As a precaution, I spent those recesses with my council. I was with them when we saw Cello pass the letter to his friend. After all that time he hadn't done it yet! Sebastien read it out loud, and from afar I recognized some of my carefully chosen words on his lips. By the time he finished, both of the boys were bent over in laughter next to the playground gate. I didn't know where to hide.

"Couple of idiots," said Kathy, indignant.

My bad advisors made me turn away without saying a word about what had just happened and, worst of all, without explaining to me how I was supposed to sit at the same table as Cello at lunch, that afternoon and all afternoons to come. How was I supposed to keep coming to school?

From what I have been able to observe, it seems that when an event hurts us there are two general tendencies in confronting it: the first being to go over it an infinite number of times, like a video we project again and again on a screen in our minds. The second is to tear apart the filmstrip and forget indefinitely the painful event. Some of us employ both techniques in the editing of our memories. I know that at first the episode of the letter to Sebastien obsessively occupied my thoughts and now, when I try to conjure it up, the details escape me. I know, for example, that I avoided the cafeteria for several days. I preferred fasting to the humiliation of another encounter. I even asked the principal to assign me to another lunch table, but since I didn't dare explain the real reasons for my request, it was refused as insubstantial. Sooner or later I had to return and somehow, with all the strength in the world, keep my head held high. Luckily, Cello never held it against me, and the only time he brought it up I pretended that it wasn't the least bit important to me. The art of craftiness has always been one of the trilobite's greatest weapons. As far as I know, Blaise never knew anything about the letter. If he did, he kept it to himself in friendly silence.

Blaise was the son of a famous French cartoon artist who lived in Paris and had lived there for years. Blaise and his mother lived in Aix, but in a much cleaner and nicer neighborhood than ours. Blaise liked reading graphic novels and was well informed about the new works as well as the classics of the genre. He was also interested in literature, but not to the same degree. Now and then we'd exchange reading recommendations, always thinking of the other's interests and tastes. I suggested he read Émile Ajar's *The Life Before Us* and *The Portrait of Dorian Gray*, but would never have lent him *The Four Daughters of Doctor March*, as I knew perfectly well that it would have disgusted him to the point of nausea. He recommended *Brave New World* by Aldous Huxley and the book by René Barjaval, but never suggested *The Hobbit*, which he kept beside his bed. My trust in Blaise was also selective. I abstained from telling him about the letter affair, but I revealed to him aspects of my life I'd never told anyone, such as how much I liked writing. I told him about how I'd earned the respect of my classmates in elementary school in Mexico by writing horror stories about them. I even read him a fragment of my diary.

"You should seriously write for real," he suggested, as if he were an expert. "Why don't you write a novel about your life?"

"But I'm only thirteen! Nothing's happened to me yet."

"Write about what is happening to you right now."

What I didn't tell him or anyone else was the story of my father. It was a way to protect us from the judgment of others. For my classmates, my father became a Lacanian psychologist who lived in Chula Vista in San Diego, California. We spent half our summers in Mexico and the other half with him. That's how I responded whenever someone asked me, but I never said so spontaneously or because I enjoyed lying. Nevertheless, that's what inspired the mimetic habit that has since governed a good part of my life. It wasn't hard to speak about San Diego. I'd been there several times for ophthalmologist consultations and to visit my aunt. But beyond describing the landscape, imagining a parallel life wasn't such an easy task. To sustain it, I needed to remember each and every one of the facts and descriptions I'd uttered previously. Any discrepancy could raise suspicions. And don't forget that my brother—even though he was in a different class and year—could contradict me with his own version of the facts. Rather than exciting, the entire situation ended up being pretty uncomfortable in the long run. To tell you the truth, I would have liked nothing more than to be finished with the pseudo-secrecy I had placed myself in. That kind of isolation—when pooled with the hormones of adolescence that were operating in my brain with cataclysmic force—had me spending entire afternoons collapsed on my mattress with my face buried in the pillow, sobbing violently and wanting to withdraw from the world. It was then my mother decided to hang green blinds from both our beds, which we could pull shut to delineate our own territory, and which we called the "simulacra of privacy." It was no longer necessary to have a flashlight under the covers in order to read, and I returned to self-gratification with the zealousness of one seeking salvation.

Like me, Blaise didn't talk a lot about his father. He idolized the man and at the same time felt an incurable resentment

toward him for his absence and separate life in Paris. From
the bitterness that crept into his smile whenever he described
supposedly happy vacations, I gathered they were as false
as my own. I, who came to know Blaise very well, avoided
asking about his father, but many of our classmates were
fans of his father's work and would often inquire, at which
point Blaise would proudly report the latest news on his
father's books, prizes, and translations that had come out
in recent months. Blaise didn't have any problem talking to
people, nor did he harbor any prejudices against the North
Africans as did many of the Franco-French students at our
school. The affluent kids didn't intimidate him, either. He
was a free spirit that way, and I guess that's why people
found him so easy to be around. For me, his friendship
was a gateway to meeting people I probably never would
have met on my own. Such was the case with a mysteri-
ous-looking girl. Her name was Sophie Roy and we met
her during the winter, shortly after it was announced that
The Cure were coming to Marseille. Blaise was into the
band and one afternoon when we were walking together,
he went up to the black-clad girl to ask if she'd heard about
the concert and if she knew the exact date. Based on her
physique, as much as the look on her face, Sophie seemed
much older than the rest of us. It was rumored—and it was
true—that she'd previously been expelled from two private
schools, and that her tenure at Jas de Bouffan was the last
chance her parents were giving her before having her committed. Every day she showed up at school dressed entirely
in black, in antique high-quality clothing. Instead of a coat
or jacket, she wore a cape like Arthur Rimbaud, whose

work we were studying that year in French Language and Literature. Underneath it, she wore an extremely tight skirt that clung to her silhouette, which was rather chubby and boasted curves that looked like they were about to burst out of the fabric. And she wore a button-down sweater, tight around her enormous breasts. Her blond and curly hair was always pulled into a chignon at the nape of her neck. Her eyes were large and pale blue, and she lined them with black kohl and a heavy coat of mascara. Her features and limbs were round and a little coarse, like those of a peasant woman or the baker from French fairy tales. There was something porcine about her extremely pug nose, which according to my brother looked like an electrical socket. A visible scar running down the length of Sophie's cheek cast doubt on the innocence of her face. Still, the general impression she gave was that of a sexy and disturbingly peculiar girl. In spite of the prejudices that a nerd such as myself could have against a girl of her appearance, Sophie was neither a cruel nor ill-intentioned person. From the start she was really friendly with us and even suggested that we go see The Cure with her and a group of friends she was gathering, friends from a different school because she didn't have any at Jas. The concert was three months away, so it cost nothing to accept the invitation and to keep hanging out in the meantime. It was in that moment, at lunchtime, that Blaise and I began to form a trio with the girl in black. Her presence never felt like an intrusion to us; on the contrary, her way of being made us feel included. Even though she lived in Éguilles, she almost never rode the school bus that took kids back to their towns, but would use public transportation to go downtown after class to spend a few hours with a former classmate of hers. When it would start to get dark, she'd take a city bus from the *gare routière*. Unlike the other girls in my class, she never judged the way I dressed, which the others considered old fashioned and unattractive. Instead, Sophie enthusiastically approved of my difference. On my way home from school one afternoon, I came across her leaning against the back gate I always went through as a shortcut.

"What are you doing here?" I asked, intrigued.

"I'm cutting class. You?"

"Going home."

Then she asked a question that terrified me and I didn't know how to react: "Can I come over?" she said.

I never brought people to our apartment and avoided mentioning the neighborhood we lived in as much as possible, since hearing its name immediately made most people suspicious. I tried to get out of it, but she wouldn't let me.

"Are you embarrassed of your house or your family?" she asked me bluntly.

Instead of answering the question, I tried to dodge it:

"It's a very dangerous neighborhood. Have you heard of Les Hippocampes?" I said, slowly pronouncing the name of the place as if it were a magic spell, knowing there wasn't anybody who hadn't read about it in the papers.

"You live there?" she cried. "Why didn't you say so! I've been wanting to go to that neighborhood for years, but I've never known anyone there."

I had no choice but to bring Sophie home with me. But the neighborhood didn't live up to her expectations. She had imagined a much darker and more forbidding place. Naturally, she complained about the smell of disinfectant and said it was disrespectful to force it on us. When we went into the apartment, Sunil was brewing a vanilla tea he'd just brought back from his island, and Sophie questioned him about all of his customs, including the caste system, things which my brother and I had observed but tactfully never asked about. With his newly acquired communist ideology, Sunil was delighted to answer her questions. The conversation became passionate but was cut off suddenly when my mom came in. With a stern face and as much friendliness as she could muster in that moment, Mom threw the intruder out and sent me to take a bath.

"I had a good time at your house," Sophie said to me the next morning, outside at recess. "Too bad your mom is so jealous."

Little by little, I realized that my friendship with Sophie was gaining me respect from the other students. I must have had something—something that no one had discovered yet—for this girl who was so much more mature and more wealthy than all the rest of us to have chosen me out of everybody. Suddenly they all wanted to find out what it was. I went downtown with her a few times, but I never had the chance to meet her other friends. Where I did get to go with her—and this I considered a huge demonstration of her trust in me—was on one of her visits to the doctor who managed—I found this out that same afternoon without any kind of preface or introduction—her detoxification therapy. It was the first time I saw her bare arms, covered in scars and needle tracks. I also heard her weight and blood pressure, and finally her age: thirteen. Same as me. For six months of her life, she went to that place every week and had to answer the same questions.

When we left the doctor's office that afternoon, we sat down in a quiet little square to have a coffee like the university students did. She told me briefly about how she had spent the summer in Aix living with an eighteen-year-old boy named Adam, but had to break up with him when she decided to quit and get clean once and for all. She never talked about it again. Nor did she tell me what the scar on her face was from. I, in turn, talked about Sebastien, whom I continued to dream about in secret, and the mortifying letter incident. Compared to her story, mine was embarrassingly childish, but she still listened to it with the same seriousness and respect with which I had listened. The visit sealed our friendship—a friendship marked by a large number of differences, but for that our few similarities became stronger. What were they? First and foremost we were outsiders, and we both had several uncomfortable secrets that couldn't be shared. We were both going through a tough time. But I was wrong to think these similarities and the tacit complicity between us also implied loyalty or some kind of commitment. This I would figure out later, not that afternoon, nor in the following days which I passed under the happy illusion of having found a true friend.

One night, while we were eating dinner with some hippie women and forty-year-olds at Lisa's house, it got into my mother to condemn my behavior: she said that ever since I had been spending time with certain friends, I had started acting like a seductress, and that my body language, the intonation in my voice, and my linguistic expressions now responded to a stereotype—the cliché of a showgirl or little pin-up doll. It is enough to analyze how I felt in those days, just a little bit, to know that nothing could have been further from reality. But, Dr. Sazlavski, if it had been true, wouldn't it have been more deserving of applause and encouragement? The ability to seduce another human being is one of the most powerful instruments a woman can acquire, better than mastering a foreign language or culinary skills. If I had actually started to practice that subtle discipline, wouldn't it have been better to let it develop fully, rather than to inhibit my attempts? Of course her friends took her side—the most attractive women hypocritically—saying they would have to educate the next generation so that we wouldn't fall into the mental prisons imposed by our consumerist society. Maybe deep down it was hard for my mother to accept a possible competitor and she preferred that I keep hunching my shoulders like a defensive little insect.

A few months later, I went to one of the first parties in my life. It was in the beach house of one of the girls from school, in the city of Martigues, twenty minutes from Aix. My mother had a few friends in Martigues and arranged to spend the evening with them so she could pick me up later. I took the trip there with Sophie, Blaise, and his mother. Behind the party house there was some kind of grotto, maybe a wine cellar at some point or an unused granary. It was decorated to look like an eighties nightclub with spinning colorful lights and dry ice. There was also a bar with enough beer and *pastis* to get you wasted. The music was typical of those years: Depeche Mode, Europa, Aha, George Michael, Prince, and Madonna, among others. Blaise, Sophie, and I took over a corner by the bar. I felt happy to be with them. If individually we were like insects on the verge of extinction, together we formed a pretty strong group. It was as if our strangest characteristics—my crossed eye, Blaise's stature, and Sophie's scar, to name a few—were actually markings we had chosen, like piercings or tattoos. At some point during the night, they played "Just Like Heaven" by The Cure, now our favorite band, and the three of us got up to dance. Our enthusiasm caught on and all of a sudden the dance floor was full of kids with dark aspirations. Sebastien was among them. He'd come to the party without his best friend Cello and his attitude seemed much less arrogant. When the song ended he came over and offered the three of us beers. He went from group to group a few times but he always came back to us. All the friendliness from him started to make me tense. I hadn't forgotten what he and his friend had put me through just six months earlier, and I didn't trust him. But at the same time, he was so attractive. His attitude that night was so different from the one he showed off around his Italian friend. How could I not want to believe him? I was thinking about it all while waiting in line for the bathroom, trying to spot him from a distance. Then I saw him dancing with Sophie to one of those romantic songs teenagers put on at parties so they can put their arms around each other. I don't really remember what the song was about. All I know is that I couldn't go into the bathroom or move anywhere. I stayed there glued to the wall like someone expecting a huge boot to stomp down on her body. Then they both disappeared. Blaise, who had remained unaware of my history with that boy, came up to me with a glass in his hand and delivered the fatal blow:

"Sophie went home with someone. I think we've lost her."

And in a way I did lose her that night. Because even though I still talked to her and stoically accepted her silence on the topic of her adventure with Sebastien, our relationship was never the same. She never offered to explain, much less apologize. Nor did she date him, not publicly at least. She didn't even mention his name. Her behavior was the same as before the night of the party, as if she had no idea what she had done. Little by little I distanced myself from her. It was almost summer break and I pretended to be studying for final exams, until one day I just stopped saying hi.

V.

Colonie de Vacances. Together those three words evoke for many French children the best times of their lives. Basically, it's summer camp organized for children of a certain age to experience community living and a little more independence than typically found at home. Many of the camps are focused on a particular interest, such as music, painting, kayaking, waterskiing, or some other outdoor activity. My brother and I had heard about these wonderful places from several of our classmates, so when Mom came to us with the idea, it didn't occur to either one of us to say no. It has to be said that most of the girls at my school had been kissed for the first time in such circumstances, which was a point in favor of my mom's plan. Even though the camps were organized by the city council, they didn't cost as little as you might think. Signing us up was a considerable investment for my mother. She also had to pay for all the accessories we needed: a single sleeping mat, a sleeping bag, a backpack for the three nights we'd be sleeping under the stars, hiking boots, a flashlight, and I can't remember how many other things. In exchange, my brother and I were promised two weeks of nonstop adventure and fun, and my mother was promised the chance to make progress on her thesis. However, I didn't know that the city council made up the camp groups according to the zones we lived in. Rather than encouraging an exchange between social classes, they preferred to keep neighbors together—as if discord among neighbors wasn't something universal, almost inherent in any given culture. That's how, one morning, my brother and I found ourselves on a bus with all the kids from our neighborhood, the ones we had been trying to avoid on the streets and in the stairwells of our building for over three years. Not in my worst nightmare had I imagined this situation. I recognized some of my classmates, including Rachida and her sister—the two girls Nathalie and I had fought years earlier—who where there with excited smiles and enormous backpacks. The bus brought us to a spot I didn't know, whose beauty I'd heard mentioned more than once, but whose name only increased my unease that morning: the Gorges of the Luberon. As the bus labored its way along the right lane of the highway, I imagined myself ambushed by several of those kids in dark caves like the throats of wolves. Luckily I wasn't traveling alone; whatever happened, my brother would be by my side. As I was thinking all this over, I looked at him in the seat next to me, his expression hopeful and calm. The poor thing was still contemplating the possibility of a dream vacation.

I can't say it was a peaceful ride. Everyone around us shouted and laughed at high decibels, including the eighteen-year-old counselor who was trying to keep them under control. Only a few kids stared out the window. I thought they must be memorizing the route, in case they'd soon have to make their escape. Nonetheless, at least on the bus, the kids didn't mess with any of us. They seemed to be concentrating on acting rowdy and socializing with their friends. There were three long weeks ahead for them to get to know—and to bully—the new kids. During the entire ride I was praying for my bunkmate to be one of the prudent and quiet girls. But when we finally arrived at the campsite, it was announced that we would sleep in groups of twenty in teepees: impressively large tents that were already set up and waiting for us in the middle of nowhere.

"When you know which tent you're in, you can put your sleeping mat and things in whatever spot you like," announced the counselor, who then started reading a list of everyone's names and the tent numbers they were assigned to. My brother and I weren't in the same tent. Things were getting worse by the minute. But he didn't seem the least bit fazed by our imminent separation. I was, however, with Rachida and Besma. I found them eagerly marking off their territory a few feet from where I had put my things. They weren't particularly hostile toward me, nor did they seem to be holding any grudges. Accustomed as they were to fighting in the street, it's likely the event occupied a very different place in their memories than it did in mine. I smiled at them to be cautious and test the waters, and to my relief they both happily returned the gesture.

"We're neighbors here too!" the older girl said.

It was a calm afternoon. When it got dark, at around ten at night, the counselors started a bonfire and we all sat around it for a few hours. I watched all the boys interacting and tried to fight off my apprehension and mistrust. I wondered if one of them might be suitable for a first kiss. Was it possible that I could grow to like someone? We would find out by the end of camp.

The kids all gradually went into their tents to curl up on their inflatable mattresses. Only a few of us silently stayed until the end. I remember that when I finally went back to my spot, I fell into a deep and peaceful sleep. I did not, however, wake the same way. Before opening my eyes I heard a short someone yelling in his underpants nearby.

"I'm so horny, you feel me? And I'm looking to screw a *meuf* even if I have to rape her!"

I heard laughter around me. Maybe because I was one of the only girls still lying down by that time, the boy moved in my direction, making suggestive movements with his pelvis. Others started to shout:

"*Z'yas va*, Pierre! Give it to her!"

It wasn't a decision. It was more like my body started acting by itself without consulting my brain: I leapt out of bed and started kicking my attacker until he was down. I only stopped when I saw his nose was bleeding. I had no idea who the boy was or what kind of a reputation he had among the others. I didn't find out until later that he was feared in our neighborhood for his brutality. Taking him down turned me into a force to be reckoned with and, at the same time, given that no one knew me, someone not to be trusted. At breakfast, kids from my tent and a neighboring tent came over to offer their friendship and share their respect.

"Honestly, we never would have guessed. Girls with glasses are usually such wusses."

"It was good you defended yourself. Next time break his nose for me."

When I didn't think anyone else was coming over, my brother came to ask if what he'd heard was true. Unlike him, not one of the counselors came to corroborate the story. They preferred to pretend nothing had happened and to go ahead with their plans.

This was followed by several uneventful days, at least where I was concerned. An altercation would suddenly break out in the middle of the constant ruckus of our voices. Whenever there was a fight, or the threat of one, a small circle of spectators would form. But things would almost immediately go back to being normal—tense but cheerful—for the group. With time, my brother learned all the names of the forty kids at camp. He took part in almost every athletic activity, such as mountain climbing and the occasional kayaking competition. I, on the other hand, carried on without adapting. Whenever invited to do something physical, I said I had a headache. I lied to the counselor and said I had my period and preferred to remain lying down for as long as possible. I'd brought three fairly long novels with me and hoped to finish them before going back to Aix. Truthfully, I was bored. A few miles from the campsite there was a pay phone, which was the destination of the impromptu walks I made several times a day. I'd call my mother, usually without reaching her, and when I finally did I would relate to her in a very dramatic voice everything repulsive about the place, including my fight in the tent with the maniac. When I was finished, she would always ask, "But you're OK, right?"

What I wanted to happen never did: to hear her say that she was coming to get me as soon as she could.

Bastille Day arrived. Before that, the camp kids had organized a few nights of dancing and cigarettes (unlike booze, smokes were allowed), during which I avoided company of any kind, despite knowing the main objective for these social gatherings was to end up going out with someone. But this time was different; it was a joint party with the camp and town, which promised more activities, greater freedom, and new people. The dance started at seven p.m., when the heat was still suffocatingly intense, and went on until after midnight. I spent more time on the dance floor than I had at any other party, dancing with anyone who asked. Two of my dance partners suggested that we get out of there and get something to drink. One of them was French and a high school student, the other was a bit older and also more handsome, a Ceuta-born Tunisian who had come to the town to work at laying bricks. I was pleasantly surprised to see them fight over me. I went with the bricklayer. We sat in the bar that was farthest from the center of town. It had a dark terrace and open tables, and there I let him kiss me until there wasn't the smallest trace of inexperience left on my lips. When the bar closed, we continued walking through the empty alleys of white cobblestone. He—whose name I don't have the courtesy to remember—was admirably decent. He never tried to force me to do something I didn't want to do. Several times he invited me to the room he was renting, but I preferred the streets and their half-lit corners. I let him touch my breasts, but my shirt stayed on. We stayed together in the street until very late. The many hours gave him enough time to tell me about his life, his parents, his childhood in Spain. Even though he spoke Spanish perfectly, French was the language we used. Then at dawn he walked me back to camp.

The counselors were furious. They scolded me and said they were going to tell my mother about my escapade. My only response for them was to shrug my shoulders a few times. I was tired that morning but in a great mood, and contrary to my ways I ended up talking at the breakfast table. I looked at my peers, especially those of Tunisian origins, with new eyes, as if they were the siblings or cousins of my momentary boyfriend. No longer did I feel the same uneasiness or mistrust. Rachida with her fatness, or Malika with her endless acne seemed more deserving of fondness than of anything else. I'd never imagined that going out with a boy could have such an effect on me, and I would probably have become a friend to one and all in the camp had my mother, alarmed by the counselor's report, not come to pick me up in her friend's car. My brother decided to stay ten more days, until the end of summer vacation, and returned enthralled by his three new friends in the building. Though in a different way, the *colonie de vacances* had helped me make friends, too. Sometimes, when heading outside, I'd run into my teepee mates. We'd greet one another with uncommon camaraderie. Some came over to tell me they'd been sorry to see me go home. Instead of making me wary, these kids now sympathized with me. I was no longer the target of their roughness, the person on which they might prey to prove their ability to start trouble. Instead, they displayed enormous vulnerability to me. I knew better than anyone that to survive in environments like my school, you needed a strong dose of courage and dignity, and the slightest affront to that dignity was worth defending with your life. In the end, in their own way, they were trilobites too.

After several years of living in Les Hippocampes—going every morning to Jas de Bouffan, eating with Cello, and spending summer vacations with the neighborhood kids—I ended up forgetting, at least partly, the world I came from. I'd become so mimetic that anyone who met me at that time would have assumed that I had either been born in Aix or had been raised there. However, that same summer, I received a significant glimpse of my country and the origins to which—sooner or later, though I didn't know it then—I would have to return. That year, Mexico was the guest country at the Festival d'Aix. For nearly three weeks, there were Mexican writers and artists walking around the streets downtown. Among those invited was Daniel Catán, the musician we had met before moving to France. He very kindly got us into many of the events, concerts, and readings. Still very present in my mind is the memory of the afternoon when on the stone steps of the Palais de Justice he introduced us to Octavio Paz who was just about to read in the auditorium. There was no time then, or after, to speak to him. We were barely able to greet him before he rushed off to go onstage. We did, however, have the chance to listen to his poetry for over an hour. On his lips the Spanish of Mexico ceased being the intimate dialect in which my mother, brother and I spoke to one another; it transformed into a malleable and precious material. Those poems spoke of poplars of water, of Pirul trees and obsidian, sugar skulls, the barrio of Mixcoac, places and things I had loved in a distant but—I understood then—not completely forgotten time. I remembered who we were, and when I did, I felt a mix of happiness and pride. As night fell, returning home through the silent streets of Aix-en-Provence, I told myself that if some day I was to write, it would have to be in this language.

Spending the rest of the summer with me must have been torture for my mother. She complained that at camp I had picked up the speech and insolence of my peers.

"Deal with it! You're the one who sent us there to get rid of us," I told her angrily.

Sometimes I knew her complaints were warranted, but there was nothing I could do about it. It was a war against the world: war of the trilobites. I had enlisted and transgressions weren't an option. My mother—by the fact of being my mother, but also because she was authoritarian and self-satisfied—wasn't one of us. She didn't realize it and did everything she could to be close to me, to build the bridge of complicity that according to her we were missing. Often her efforts backfired. I remember, for example, one Sunday morning while we were eating breakfast together at the kitchen table, she casually asked if I had already had sex with a man.

"It's normal for it to happen, you know? But when it does, I want you to tell me."

She was, I believe, right to think I had—after what had happened at camp—but she was not right to ask me about it, much less to do it straight-out like she did. Her apparently unconcerned tone sounded off-key and obviously fake.

I pushed the table and jumped up from my seat. Before stamping off to my room I had enough time to tell her to mind her own business. It wasn't the only time she would try to be my friend, but, as it was that Sunday, all her attempts would be rejected. At the beginning of September, one week before classes were about to start, my mother announced that she was sending me back to Mexico. According to her, another stint with my grandmother would help to keep me in line during this very rebellious age. My brother would stay with her. So I went back to Mexico City, finishing the 3ème to then start my first year of high school at the Liceo Franco-Mexicano. My classmates would never again be the kids from the outskirts—the kids of the *banlieues*—but the children of businessmen, diplomats, and French expatriates living in our country.

No, Doctor Sazlavski. I don't think I'm holding onto any resentment toward my mother. But I do recognize a feeling of bitterness for all that our relationship could have been but was not, nor ever will be, despite the good moments we share every so often, despite the complicity that unites us on occasion. Sometimes, especially when she has one of her crises of hypochondria that always make me falter, I imagine the day of her death and glimpse the unfathomable void that will be left in my life when it happens. It's as if the obsessive Captain Ahab were suddenly told his whale was beached forever, and he could never chase it again. Like *Moby Dick*, our story is also a story of love, love and a failure to connect.

VI.

Anyone who has read the first part of this book carefully might imagine that living with my grandmother again would terrify me. It's true, at first I took the decision as an excessive sentencing imparted by my mother and proof that she didn't care about me at all. I was also surprised the old woman agreed to have me spend a year in her house after our first round of living together, also knowing I was at the worst stage, according to tradition, that kids go through. But contrary to all my expectations, the second time around wasn't as unbearable as the first. Apart from the issue of table manners, my grandmother showed me polite indifference, which made daily life tedious but peaceful. Only the servant who was in charge of the cooking and cleaning shared the ramshackle house with us. My grandmother and I almost never crossed paths, not even at dinner sometimes. Nobody made sure I got up in time for school, or that I ate well; nobody washed my clothes or ironed my uniform; nobody asked me indiscreet questions. Living there was like living alone, except for one important detail: under no set of circumstances was I allowed to leave the house unaccompanied.

Unlike Jas de Bouffan, with its gardens and athletic fields, my new school resembled a prison. I knew that first-hand. Another noticeable difference was the color of the students; as many students as teachers were white, at least 80 percent—odd in an essentially indigenous country. The superintendent, however, was not white, and neither were the janitors or lunch ladies, and this heightened the contrast more. There were a handful of Muslims, the sons and daughters of diplomats. To an outsider like me, it was all so obvious, but to those who'd been living for years in the Mexican bourgeois community, it was apparently insignificant. Classes started at eight and ended at six, a pretty long day compared to the national schools. There were some free hours halfway through. All subjects except gym were taught in a foreign language. My French—the only French I knew—was that of the *banlieues* of the south of France. Mexicans didn't realize what I was speaking (they were impressed by my pronunciation and strange vocabulary); the French and Maghreb did, and even though both were horrified to listen to me, they left me alone. My compatriots, on the other hand, were constantly asking me about my family, what I did on weekends, and where I bought my clothes. They were determined to fit me into one of their narrow social categories. Of the school's implicit codes, clothing and school supplies were particularly important. The more French brand-name clothing a girl had, the more fancy pens in her backpack, the better she was regarded in that small society. I remember several of those kids had at least one gold-tipped Montblanc, which they'd proudly glide across their Claire Fontaine notebooks. Where clothing was concerned, Burlington argyle socks were, and I have no clue why, the most highly regarded. Overall, style at our school matched what the French often call *BCBG*, a nickname meaning acceptable within a conformist and boring bourgeoisie. When at last they had gathered enough information about me, the neighborhood where I lived, and what my mother did for a living, they decided the appropriate label for me was "hobo," and they had no qualms about calling me that, which in their way of seeing the world was an insult. The contempt was mutual. To me, all those short-sighted snobs were as soft and bland as sausages. Later on, as time passed, I discovered that among them there were also warmhearted people, but early on I was at war and unwilling to seek anyone out, blinded by my own prejudices.

The school bus came for me every morning at six. I'd go out to wait for it by the front door, freezing to death, with a still-dark sky above my head. The ride was two hours spent locked up with thirty half-awake kids of different ages, students in elementary, middle, and high school. The environment in the bus was like a miniature reproduction of what took place at our school and in the world in general: some bullied, others were picked on. There were the arrogant and the insecure. The whites would always start in on the dark ones, while the blonds looked on from above with indifference. I was too old to be a target of the bullies, but they didn't look kindly on me either. I didn't talk to anybody, and nobody came over to talk to me.

In Mexico, social classes rival the caste system in India. If chance wills for a child to be born into a high-class family, it's likely she will spend very little time among the masses, and only in exceptional places on exceptional occasions, at the soccer stadium or in the Main Square on Independence Day. Jail is a place of encounter. After a year at the Reclusorio, my father was transferred to another prison on the west side of the city known as Santa Marta Catitla. He remained there for four years and always referred to it as "The Palace of Iron," alluding to a luxury department store of the same name. What I know about his life during that time isn't much. I do know he exercised daily and with discipline. He started exercising when his thrombosis was at its worst and a friend dragged him to the bars. I also know he taught math, logic, and grammar in the education programs they ran for adults, and that he truly enjoyed it. His sentence was reduced a few months because he taught. I was surprised he didn't take piano or guitar classes as he had in earlier periods in his life. Maybe there weren't many teachers, or the teachers they had weren't very good. Instead he threw himself deep into reading Husserl and his phenomenology, the gist of which he's tried in vain to explain to me more than once. In prison he also discovered the books of Gurdjieff and Ouspensky. They were a great support to him during the hardest times of his stay. He told me about a few people he met: an Italian named Paolo and a composer accused of involuntary manslaughter for killing an old woman. I also know that he learned how to work with natural resins, since sometimes he sent a few of his pieces to us, me and my brother, to our home in Aix. They came to us like weird meteorites from a different dimension. Strange as it may seem, my father got himself a girlfriend while he was inside. She was a rather beautiful woman he'd met in his days as a psychoanalyst. She was a psychologist herself and taught graduate courses at the National University. Her name was Rosaura. Like him, she was tall, slim, and above all a very good person. I don't want to imagine the conjugal visits in there.

In the year I returned to live with my grandmother, I saw my father somewhat frequently. Rosaura would pick me up in her car once or twice a month, always on a weekend. On the way, we'd talk about movies and literature and we'd reassure each other, saying that Dad would get out any day now. Even though his sentence was almost up, the truth is that it was impossible to know what date the authorities would approve. Her presence made me feel like I was with a friend. On one of these mornings, she gave me a Milan Kundera novel, *The Unbearable Lightness of Being*, which I devoured in short time. The tedium of my daily life was such that those outings were the greatest adventure I was afforded then.

During our visits, my father would ask me about school. He wanted to know if I paid close attention in class, if I liked the subjects, if I was getting good grades, if I got along with the other students. I'd go on and on describing in detail how insufferable and shallow my classmates were, but he didn't like me talking about other people that way. He told me that no matter where you are it's possible to find an ally, and the more hostile the surroundings, the more important it is to develop true friendships.

"Promise me that next time you come, you'll have made a friend."

My only choice was to agree, but it was three months before I came back.

The agreement I made with my father wasn't the reason I got close to Camila. Our friendship came about as most do: organically, almost surreptitiously. She lived near me and also spent hours on the school bus in the morning and in the stifling heat of the afternoon—hours in which the last thing one wants to do is strike up a conversation. She came over one morning to ask me if she could borrow the book I was reading when I had finished it. I'd barely noticed her before. She was short and sour-faced. Her light brown hair was cut short like a boy's, and she almost always wore big sweaters or athletic clothes. At first sight, she wasn't much to look at. But when I came to really know her, I understood that I had before me one of the strongest personalities I would ever meet in my life. That morning, I said yes to her question and then immediately stuck my nose back in the book, but she was excited and kept on talking. The book I was holding in my hands, *The Merchant of Venice*, belonged to the library of my deceased grandfather and was in Spanish. She had, she told me, read almost every Shakespeare play in French, and all she was missing was this play and it wasn't in the school library. She told me her favorite at the moment was *Macbeth* and I had to read it to know the playwright.

Camila wasn't like the other students at our high school. She didn't speak in a posh accent or end every sentence as if it were a question. Like me, she was in the *seconde* but in a different section, and she was at least two years older than her classmates. She also had a stepfamily, and she lived with her mother, a very political woman, a militant leftist who'd been involved in hijacking a plane in Chile. On the other hand, her father, by her own description, was a weakling who couldn't find suitable work. Lautaro, her older brother, preferred to take the metro to school so he wouldn't have to put up with the eternal and soporific bus ride. She didn't like mediators; she went herself to parent-teacher conferences to discuss her academic progress and behavioral issues. When we became friends, she took care of the necessary paperwork to switch into my class, a move I was infinitely grateful for. From then on, we sat together in the back of the room. She wasn't a bad person or a rebel without a cause, as some people believed, but simply a teenager of extraordinary lucidity mixed with deep bitterness and rather dark sense of humor. She made fun of everyone and could make anyone laugh at themselves. I remember so well the time the math teacher, a woman with pronounced lordosis, while teaching us the x-axis and y-axis declared that her own posture was perpendicular to the floor. Camila burst into a loud and contagious laugh. "Miss!" she blurted, "how can you say that? Have you looked in the mirror?" I remember she also came up with a nickname for the French teacher who had a habit of scratching his pubic hair with his right hand. She called him "the guitarist." She did her homework ten minutes before class. Often she'd copy all of it from my notebook. Her bad grades were a product of boredom. Unlike me, her parents let her wander throughout the entire city. We never saw each other outside school, but we'd speak for several hours over the phone on weekends. Camila knew every student at school and got along with all of them. She didn't share her mother's prejudices about social class. The only topic that made her serious and emotional was Pinochet's dictatorship in Chile.

Even though she became fond of me right away, Camila had other friends I had to share her with, her "best friends." It was hard for me to accept it but in the end I had no choice. The two girls were Yael and Xitlali, French Mexicans who had lived in the country almost all their lives. Xitlali was the only daughter of a talented architect and a French advertising agent. The main part of their house was exclusively reserved for her and her friends. It was where she was going to sleep with her boyfriend as soon as she decided to. The house had a little garden for growing marijuana for the family. Yael, on the other hand, was a Polanco princess who lived alone with her father. Among her greatest feats was that she had run away from home more than once to spend the weekend in Acapulco with her many lovers. She had always been found thanks to a credit card that she used to finance her drug purchases and other expenses. Her father had been accused in several countries of illegal diamond trafficking, but he always managed to miraculously get out of prison. Although they had complete trust in Camila and her criteria for choosing friends, the girls considered me a little childish, and next to them there's no question I was:

I'd never been to a dance club, I'd never tried any halluci-nogens, I'd never slept with a guy, and it didn't look like my situation was going to change in the near future.

Gradually, by answering when she called, my grand-mother grew used to Camila's presence. One evening, I asked permission to have dinner at Camila's house and my grandmother gave it to me. I assured her that Camila's parents would bring me home. The truth is that it never would have crossed Camila's mind to invite me to her house then; her mother was a permanent nervous wreck in a perpetual shouting match with her husband. Nor did I have any intention of meeting her family; my goal was to secure a new dimension of freedom so I could go out into the city. With that permission, Camila and I went to Xitlali's for dinner. Yael joined us later on. It was then I had the chance, not only to see the famous plant, but also to partake of its harvest, clean and dry, in a lovely Huichol pipe that according to our host was most appropriate for my introduction to the sacred weed. At first I didn't feel the effect of the cannabis, but as time passed and with-out really noticing it, my tongue became abnormally loose to the point that I ended up spilling everything I'd kept bottled up for years. I'd smoked a truth serum without suspecting it. What prompted my blabbering was a com-ment from Yael, who had the nerve to state that I'd made it to fifteen years old without learning anything about life. To show her she was mistaken, I told her that I knew the prisons as well as she did and had visited my father there a bunch of times. I told them about my romance with the Tunisian bricklayer on Bastille Day. I described my fistfight against the rapist-in-training. And to Camila's delight, I spoke of Ximena. Before finishing, I extoled the dignity and resistance of all trilobites, to whose lineage the three of us belonged, of that they should be absolutely sure.

When I finished speaking, the girls stared at me with shock on their faces: the marijuana had transformed me.

"You were brilliant," Camila congratulated me on the metro ride home. "I've never seen you like that." But I felt the indescribable shame of someone who has just betrayed herself, spitting out all her secrets. Nonetheless, Doctor, despite the aftermath I also felt an incredible lightness—the same I've come to experience while telling you everything. Silence, like salt, only seems to be weightless. In reality, if one allows time to dampen it, it grows heavy as an anvil.

The other day, while we were peacefully eating dinner in the garden at my mother's country house, a completely unexpected situation arose. Over dessert, my mother looked at me with the curiosity of a journalist and asked if I was writing anything at the moment. Coming from someone else, this is the kind of question I'd normally consider tactless. But since she was the one asking, and it happened often, it felt wildly impolite. Dr. Sazlavski, you and I both know perfectly well that I haven't written anything in over a year and a half, except a few articles and critical pieces that let me make some money, but I didn't feel like admitting as much that night. So I remained silent for a few seconds, waiting for a response from the crickets whispering their curses hidden in the grass, then I answered without giving it too much thought.

"I'm writing a novel about my childhood." Then it was my mother who took a while to respond.

"I'm sure you're talking badly about me," she said. "You have all your life."

To go out at night. This was the main goal in the underground struggle I waged against my grandmother. She never let me go to any parties with Camila and her friends. It's not that she particularly mistrusted them; it's just that she didn't know them well enough. Before giving me an answer she would exhaustively ask: Whose house was I going to? What was the address and phone number where she could reach me? Who was I going there with? Who was coming back with me? And what time would I be coming home? I prepared my answers as if I was training for an oral exam and still, even after thinking it over for a few days, my grandmother would always come to the same conclusion: "I prefer you don't go"—until the day I decided to change my strategy. One night, as my grandmother slept in her bedroom, I followed in the footsteps of my dear Betty and from the roof of the house crossed over to the neighbor's terraced roof and climbed down to the street on the back staircase. Camila was waiting for me in a car a few feet away. I made it out unscathed, except for a few scratches and some dust on my clothes. It was the only way I would be able to go to a dance club in the capital—to a huge and dark place with red velvet seats, where people danced and girls dressed in skimpy clothing tried to comment on what was going on around them over the volume of the music. To get in, I had to lie about my age, but once inside they served me as much alcohol as I wanted, not once asking for my ID. In true Mexican fashion, Camila's friend treated us to drinks and cigarettes. It would have been a perfect night if that dive had enforced an age cap. With two gins in me already, in the midst of the dry ice and as if out of a hallucination, I recognized my grandmother's silhouette, her typical dark clothing and fluffy white hair. She'd taken a taxi and was there to rescue me from the fires of hell. Before she reached the table, I gathered my things and met her on the dance floor. I left without saying good-bye, hoping to avoid a scene and anyone else spotting my grandmother.

Despite my prejudices against all the students at our high school, over time I noticed that in generations other than my own there were also certain specimens whose originality and strength were thrilling. Such was the case with Antolina, a very pretty-faced girl who was characterized by an extremely short height most often referred to as dwarfism, and who nevertheless possessed more self-confidence and assuredness than I had ever dreamed of myself, and which made her look particularly beautiful—so much so that in one of those stupid contests the students organized year after year, in which they hand out superlatives such as Fattest, Sexiest, and Dumbest, Antolina was declared by the vast majority of votes to be the most attractive girl in our school. Though we never exchanged more than two words at recess—unlike her, I suffered from a paralyzing shyness—watching her interact became a source of inspiration to me. It was years before I discovered the secret of her beauty, which I admired in silence as one might gaze upon a musician performing an exceptionally complicated piano piece with the stirring talent granted by virtuosity. Later on, I learned that her mother, actress and muse to Alejandro Jodorowski, had the same characteristics Antolina did, and I told myself that maybe it was a secret passed on from generation to generation, and I didn't have a right to claim it.

These are, without a doubt, the memories of my childhood and adolescence all entangled in an intricate snare with infinite possible interpretations of which not even I am aware. Sometimes I think that removing the heavy covering that separates me from the cesspool and reliving the pains of the past does nothing but reinforce the feeling of unease that leads me to your office. I also wonder if your silence hasn't fostered the uncertainty in which I now find myself. Sometimes I succumb to doubting the whole story, as if it's not what I lived but a tale I've told myself again and again an infinite number of times. At that thought, the feeling of bewilderment I have becomes abyssal, hypnotic, a kind of existential precipice inviting me to take a definitive leap.

At a family reunion that year, I met one of my second cousins who would also play an important role in my life. Her name was Alejandra and she was the daughter of Aunt Sara, my mother's cousin. Alejandra was as unsatisfied as I was when it came to school and the tedium of family life. Both of us had a feeling that the world was much bigger and more exciting than what the tiny crack we had access to allowed us to see, and for that reason we immediately identified with each other. The day we met, we decided to sign up for a theater workshop held at the Casa de la Cultura de Coyoacán.

Aleja, that's what I called her, had a car for moving about city as she pleased, and when she couldn't borrow it, she knew how to seize the same freedom using public transportation. After our workshop, we'd spend a few hours in the streets and plaza of the area, which in those days attracted some rather strange misfits. Artisans, mimes, street musicians, intellectuals, and bohemians could be found there in an imitation of what the plaza in Montmartre once was. We immediately fell in with a group of friends made up of those we'd run into in the evenings and on some weekends, people who would have horrified our families with their appearances alone, not to mention their habits—they drank and smoked profusely—and vocabulary. But these characteristics were genuinely fascinating to us. Besides our immense affection for each other, one of the advantages of our friendship was that my grandmother believed Aleja to be as modest and well behaved as her mother thought me. So as long as we were together, they had nothing to worry about. Luckily, my aunt and uncle left the city on weekends, sure that we'd be spending Friday night at home watching Disney movies. Because of this, Aleja and I were able to go to parties, the likes of which I'd never known before, full of artists of every age and hosted in enormous, illustrious houses, such as Indio Fernández's and Malinche's near Plaza de la Conchita. Smoking and drinking became a habit that would take us years to kick.

The more time I spent with my cousin in our new social milieu, the more difficult getting along at high school seemed to be. In those days of taking sides and searching for an identity all mine, I adopted the style of Coyoacán's bohemians in order to make my ideological differences perfectly clear. This is why, instead of the Burlington argyle socks, I started to wear long lightweight skirts imported from India, white linen pants, and artisanal leather sandals. I also wore a felt hat and men's vests borrowed from my grandfather's closet, while Aleja stealthily took from her father's suits. Scarves and silver-pendent earrings were an essential part of my wardrobe. I decided to show off my eccentricity, which expressed another way might have come off as unintentional or out of control. To accept it this way was a demonstration of strength. The more radical I became in my weird hippiness, the more I grew apart from Camila, who at that moment was undergoing an inverse metamorphosis: very close to Yael, my friend was starting to imitate Polanco style and habits, not only different from but opposite in every way to what I was doing.

This morning, while getting ready to bring my son to nursery school, my mother called. She always manages to call at the worst times.

"I was up all night, thinking about your famous novel. You know I can sue you for slander?"

Later, at around eleven-thirty, my brother Lucas, who almost always ignores my calls because he's so busy, rang my cell phone while I was keeping busy watering the moribund plants in my study.

"Mom's already told me about your autobiography." After that he let out a kind of chuckle, adding, "Even though she hasn't read it, she says she'll take you to court for defamation."

"Of course she hasn't read it! I haven't even started writing it."

"Don't worry. I calmed her down by telling her to be patient and wait for the movie version. I told her, you never know, it could make a fortune."

I set the watering can on the ground and hung up the phone. For the first time in over a year and a half, I sat down at the computer to write with gusto, determined to make this "famous novel" a reality. I would finish it even if I was sued or whatever else. It would be a short and simple account. I wouldn't tell anything I didn't believe to be true.

As in other times, I found company and complicity in the space of reading. I decided to move on from the French canon we were taught in high school to search among more contemporary writers. I dedicated myself to tracking down authors the same way I found my friendships then—authors in a war against social conventions and lovers of marginality. In those days, I read with true devotion the books of the Beatnik movement. More than William Burroughs and Charles Bukowski, I identified with the novels of Kerouac and poetry of Allen Ginsberg, whose biography impressed me enormously. I felt especially inspired by some lines he wrote right before deciding to quit his job as an advertising agent and to face up to the fact that he was in love with Peter Orlovsky. They are the lines I chose to be the epigraph to my book. Like him, I also dreamed of accepting myself, even though at that point in time I still didn't know exactly what closet I hoped to come out of.

Mom returned from France a little before the end of the year, just when I had found a balance in my daily life. Right away I knew her presence would bring nothing good. Despite everything and our occasional arguments, my grandmother and I had established a distant, harmonious cohabitation in that enormous house in which we rarely crossed paths. Mom arrived with the intention of supervising everything she hadn't been in control of for almost nine months. To this end, she rifled through my report cards and the remarks my teachers wrote about me; she analyzed my clothing and didn't withhold commenting on it; and of course, she confiscated all her belongings from my closet. She also badgered me about my hair and cigarette breath. With her detective's zeal, it wasn't long before she realized that the theater workshop in Coyoacán was a cover for maintaining close ties to that which, in her words, made up "the world of ruffians." As with sex, Mom had given several very liberal speeches about the consumption of marijuana.

"If you want to try it someday I'm not going to stop you, but I'd prefer if you did it with me," she'd said more than once, convinced that I'd be delighted to share my transgressive experience with her. Now that I had finally tried it, marijuana fell into the same category as coke, morphine, and other destructive substances against which she would carry on a war to the death.

One Friday, when Aleja and I returned to her house keenly intoxicated, we discovered that her parents hadn't gone to the country as usual. At my mother's urging—my mother was also there—they had stayed home in the living room waiting for us to come back at three in the morning. It was impossible to cover up the state we were in with a lie. They could tell as soon as we walked in. That night, they threatened us with fifteen days in a juvenile detention center so we could see up-close the risks our behavior was courting. The attitude of all three was so serious, but also so frenzied at the same time that it didn't occur to either one of us to question their words. We had no choice but to stay on a tight leash for a few months. In that time, I was able to boost my grades on our final exams and thus overcome the imminent risk of being left back a year.

At last I've returned to writing with discipline. It's a regenerative and invigorating sensation, like eating hot soup when down with the flu. Every morning, after dropping my son off at nursery school, I go to the same café. I have my table and my favorite drink. Those are my two superstitions. If the table is occupied, I wait until it's free before starting. I don't know if I'm fulfilling my goal of sticking to the facts but it doesn't matter anymore. Interpretations are entirely inevitable and, to be honest, I refuse to give up the immense pleasure I get from making them. Perhaps, when I finally finish it, for my parents and brother this book will be nothing but a string of lies. I take comfort in thinking that objectivity is always subjective.

It's strange, but ever since I started with this, it feels like I'm disappearing. Not only have I realized how intangible and volatile all these events are—most cannot be proven—but there is also something physical taking place. In certain absolutely indispensible moments, my limbs give me a strangely disturbing sensation, as if they belong to a person I don't know.

When her obsessive opposition to marijuana at last calmed down, my mother started campaigning for a new cause that, yet again, had to do directly with me. After confirming with a doctor that I was past the growing stage (I was more or less the same size then as now), she felt it was the opportune moment to organize the event she had been awaiting for ten years: the operation on my right eye. From what she explained to me, she had been saving up since I was born to be able to cover the costs of surgery in the best hospital for cornea transplants in the United States. According to her research, this hospital was in Philadelphia. Her idea was to bring me there as soon as school let out and to settle in and wait for a donor. But, Doctor, these plans didn't take into account one somewhat relevant factor: my opinion.

So when—instead of the florid words of gratitude and agreement she was expecting to hear—my lips pronounced an unequivocal "No," Mom was left speechless. But even then, she didn't stop. It wasn't in her nature to throw in the towel in any circumstance, and so she went ahead with her undertaking. At the end of the day, I was a minor and by law had to do as she said. To provoke her, I explained that I liked my Quasimodo looks and sticking to them was my way of going against the establishment.

"Don't talk nonsense," she responded. "This isn't about the establishment or even about looks, but about regaining the vision in one of your eyes. Have you ever considered what would happen if you were to lose the other one?"

I now suspect that behind my revolutionary arguments was hiding a more powerful force: the terrible fear of possible failure—that is, if the operation were unsuccessful, or even disastrous. You have to admit, my mother was speaking as a pillar of common sense. On our value scale, health has always come before beauty. To let my eye become completely paralyzed was to not only let all her efforts go down the drain—the childhood exercises, the torture from the patch, the atropine drops—but to forsake the proper functioning of my body.

So I finished high school and traveled with my mother to Philadelphia. It was the hottest summer in my memory, with temperatures higher than those of the dog days in Aix. I remember how it felt to say good-bye to my friends at the airport; I wouldn't be the same when I came back. It was just the two of us traveling. We would sleep in a hotel at first, then while waiting for the day of the transplant, we would stay in a pretty rented apartment we had already reserved.

The doctor my mother had been in contact with from Mexico was named Isaac Zaidman. We went to visit him the day we arrived. He was an older man whose white beard made him look like a rabbi. He gave me the routine exam that I knew—and still know—by heart, and asked me the same old questions about my history and my family's genetic history without finding any convincing answers. He optimistically nodded when we explained all the exercising my eye had been put through in the first part of my childhood, then he conducted several exams using specialized devices I had never seen before to measure the activity of my optic nerve and the shape of my lens. He explained that it might take a few weeks for the cornea to come in, as most likely they would have to transport it from a different city. I had heard talk of the transplant ever since I was little, but a few days before it was actually going to happen the prospect of a piece of someone else's body being sewn into mine stressed me out to no end. While carrying out the studies on me, the doctors in the lab looked positively enthusiastic. So much stimulation during my childhood had no doubt had a positive effect on my eye's development. During the time it took them to deliver the results from the exams, my mother and I walked around the city's museums. There was a Mondrian exhibit at the Philadelphia Museum of Art. We also saw stunning oil paintings by Paul Klee and the sculptures at the Rodin Museum. What I liked best was our visit to Poe's house in Spring Garden, now the Edgar Allen Poe National Historic

Site, after which I reread in English *Extraordinary Stories* and some poems, including "The Raven."

We visited the house of the writer the day before the definitive appointment with the doctor, and the combination of those two events made me have a particularly strange dream that night. In the dream, I entered the operating room but stayed awake for a long time. I watched the doctor cut into my eye, very slowly, with a razor like the one in the film *Un Chien Andalou*. Once my eye was gaping open, the doctor removed from it a very small object. It was a red seed no bigger than two centimeters long, like a bean seed. In the bottom part of the seed, where there is usually a seam, there was an embedded miniature marble sculpture of a white elephant exquisitely carved and serving as a lid. With enormous care, the doctor's long and delicate fingers sealed in latex gloves managed to lift the sculpture and extract from the seed a tiny parchment that I could see in his hand, and I recognized several letters of the Hebrew alphabet. I knew this paper explained the reasons why I was born with the peculiarity in my eye, and I was anxious for the doctor to tell me what it said. But instead of reading it to me, he let go of the parchment and it was carried off forever by a sudden gust of wind.

"Nobody except God has the right to know the truth," he said, making him worthy of all my rancor and hate.

The next day, when we arrived at the doctor's office, Dr. Isaac Zaidman greeted us with a huge smile on his lips. He congratulated my mother on the results of the first analyses: thanks to our exercises and despite all the years I hadn't used it, my optic nerve functioned wonderfully. The report on the lens wasn't so encouraging. The retina seemed to be totally stuck to it, which greatly complicated the extraction of the cataract. In short, if we cut there, we ran the risk of emptying all the liquid out of the eye and turning it into a raisin. That is why he completely advised against the operation. Instinctively, I looked at my mother. When the doctor pronounced these words, her throat moved very noticeably as if she were swallowing an enormous bone. As he saw us off, he kept smiling.

"Maybe we'll see each other again," he said in a mysterious voice from the doorframe, winked at me. I left more worried about Mom than my optic future. Despite our constant difficulties, it bothered me to make her unhappy. I feared she would get depressed again and cry every evening like she had during a period I've already recounted, so I tried to palliate the news with my best attitude, not allowing myself to figure out how I really felt. Months later, I learned that the name Isaac means "he who laughs," and that's how I still remember the doctor, surreptitiously laughing as fate had that day at the exercises and ointments, at my mother's savings, and at all our hopes which for years had been centered on that moment.

Mom and I spent the next three days shopping in Washington DC, happily squandering some of those useless savings on the most basic of female therapies for curing frustration. We also visited the National Gallery of Art. I remember in particular a huge exhibit of Picasso and Braque paintings. I focused on the asymmetrical women both painters portrayed, whose beauty resided precisely in imbalance. I thought a lot about blindness as a possibility.

I also thought of Antolina. After three days of exhausting every sale at the malls, we went home. I wasn't wrong to think I wouldn't be returning to Mexico City the same. In that week and a half an important change had taken place in me, even though it wasn't immediately clear. My eyes and my vision were the same but I saw differently. At last, after a long journey, I decided to inhabit the body where I was born, in all its peculiarities. When all is said and done, it is the only thing that belongs to me and ties me to the world, and allows me to set myself apart.

Things on the outside had also radically changed in our absence: the morning of my second appointment with Dr. Zaidman, and without forewarning, my father was released. Even though Mom called my grandmother's house several times on the trip, they never told us anything. They wanted it to be a surprise. We met him at the arrival gate at the airport. He had no bag and no suitcase, much less flowers in hand. He was like an apparition. On his face there was a childlike smile and not a sign of forced manners. He wore the blessed and somewhat dopey smile of someone who has just regained his freedom and doesn't know what to do with it. His appearance was also one of fate's jokes, as if fate's intention was to tell us that not all hopes are fulfilled as expected.

After everything, Dr. Sazlavski, my doubts don't make me so afraid. There is something healthy and good, as well as maddening, in calling into question the events of a life and the veracity of my own history. Maybe it's normal, this continuous sense of the ground falling out from below. Maybe all the certainties that I have always carried about myself and the people around me are becoming blurred now. My own body that for years constituted my only believable link to reality now feels like a vehicle that's breaking down, a train I've been riding all this time, going on a very fast trip toward inevitable decline. Many of the people and places that used to make up my recurrent landscapes have disappeared with astonishing ease, and many of those remaining, through accentuating their neuroses and facial gestures so fiercely, have turned into caricatures of who they once were. The bodies where we are born are not the same bodies that we leave the world in. I'm not only referring to the infinite number of times our cells divide, but to more distinctive features—these tattoos and scars we add with our personality and convictions, in the dark, by touch, as best we can, without direction or guidance.

About the Author

The New York Times described GUADALUPE NETTEL's acclaimed English-language debut, *Natural Histories* (Seven Stories 2014), as "five flawless stories." A Bogotá 39 author and *Granta* "Best Untranslated Writer," Nettel has received numerous prestigious awards, including the Gilberto Owen National Literature Prize, the Antonin Artaud Prize, the Ribera del Duero Short Fiction Award, and most recently the 2014 Herralde Novel Prize. *The Body Where I Was Born* is her highly anticipated first novel to appear in English. She lives and works in Mexico City.